As Long As It's Big

JOHNS HOPKINS: POETRY & FICTION
John T. Irwin, *General Editor*

THE JOHNS HOPKINS UNIVERSITY PRE
Baltimore

John Bricuth

AS LONG AS IT'S

ig

A
Narrative
Poem

This book has been brought to publication with the generous assistance
of the Albert Dowling Trust and the J. G. Goellner Endowment.

The Johns Hopkins University Press
2715 North Charles Street
Baltimore, Maryland 21218-4363

www.press.jhu.edu

Library of Congress Cataloging-in-Publication Data

Bricuth, John, 1940–
    As long as it's big : a narrative poem / John Bricuth.
        p. cm. — (Johns Hopkins, poetry and fiction)
    ISBN 0-8018-8245-1 (hardcover : alk. paper)
    1. Divorce—Fiction. 2. Children—Death—Fiction. 3. Suicide
victims—Family relationships—Poetry. I. Title. II. Series
PS3552.R454A93 2005
811'.54—dc22   2005007792

Portions of *As Long As It's Big* first appeared in the following magazines:
Section I in the *Southwest Review* 85, no. 2 (2000); Section II, III, and IV
(part 2) in *Boulevard;* and Section IV (Part 1) in *Point of Contact*. The
author wishes to thank the editors of these magazines and gratefully
acknowledges their permission to reprint. In addition, Section I was
given the Elizabeth Matchett Stover Award in Poetry for the best poem
published in the *Southwest Review* in the year 2000, for which the author
wishes to thank the editor of the magazine and the donor of the award,
Jerry Stover.

Once Again, For Meme, My Beloved

THE FOLLOWING is a long narrative poem about marriage that's set in the judge's chambers of a divorce court, where one last attempt is being made to save the marriage of Mr. and Mrs. Fish through a reconciliation hearing. The participants are the judge (addressed as sir and your honor), Mr. and Mrs. Fish, Mr. Fish's lawyer Mr. Fox, Mrs. Fish's lawyer Mr. Bird, Mrs. Fish's sister Gert, and the bailiff Mr. Biggs. While some of the characters in the present poem bear the same names as those in my previous poem *Just Let Me Say This About That,* they play entirely different roles in the present work, though at times they exhibit a continuity of voice and personality with their appearances in the earlier poem. The judge's remarks are printed in italics, the other characters' speeches are in roman.

I, II, III : *Allegro*

IV, V, VI : *Largo*

VII : *Presto*

I What's that thumping rumpus in the hall—
Smack and slap, body bump, sudden
Thud? There, Fox. Hear that? Sounded like

A muffled grunt followed by a swallowed
Groan. I swear, don't folks around these parts
Know yet the space outside a judge's chamber's

Sacrosanct, inviolate, interdict?
Not, of course, that lots of folks now'days'd
Know those words offhand. That's why last spring

I had the bailiff make a sign for spouses
Lately on the outs in big block letters,
Read: NO SLAPPING, PUNCHING, KICKING,
    BUTTING,

Then below, set in smaller type:
No Scratching, Biting, Cursing, Spitting, meant,
As you might guess, Fox, for the fairer sex.

Call me foolish, call me plain old-fashioned,
I simply can't abide, Bird, spitting in
A woman, no. Nor for that matter spitting

On a woman. Name a gent you know'd
Let that pass without a word? No, don't.
I'm sure you could. Instead, consider, boys,

The beauty of the sign, one phrase forbids
Them both. There now! that racket in the hall
Is back. You, Fox, just duck outside, see what

The trouble is, then tell the weary couples
Waiting there to have their vows sawed off,
Their passports reinstated, Hey! I'm getting

Really fed up with this noise. This random
Racket, Fox, infects the scholar's cell,
Invades the noon's repose, and virtually

Insures I'll three-putt every green. You tell
Them that. You tell them if the judge once walks
Among them, Fox, they'll think those thankless years

Spent married to some squirt who picks his nose
Or cracks his gum, some skirt whose underpants
Are like a flag were boring dress rehearsals—

Run-throughs really—next to what's in store
Once I vault my desk, don my robes,
And do my shaky dance, which is to say,

If I come through that door, I'll be all over
Them like stink on poop. You tell them that.
No, better yet, on second thought, say, Fox,

"Like stink on ice cream." They'll get the picture anyway
And that polite locution better
Suits the bench's moral aura. Now, Fox,

You see what I expect? Step out, find
The facts, make your threats, then beat it back
On cat feet with their fretful cries of "Fie!"—

Another contretemps caught in time,
Contained, and then dispersed by equal parts
Quiet menace and personal charm. Meanwhile,

I'll sit here quizzing Mr. Bird who more
Than likely represents some helpless soul
Encountered for the first time slumped outside,

Snoring on a bench, what you might call
A drive-by client, Fox, a baffled citizen
Whose self-inflicted head wound of a mouthpiece

More than anything suggests how desperate
Is his knowledge of the law (though not so
Dire as his first taste of marriage). So, Fox,

Hop it. And you there, Bird, stand fast. No way
It's just some client getting jammed brings
You out this early, no. I'd bet my head

On that. You're here so we can have a little
Talk, so you can wheedle, make that "weasel,"
Some concession, slight advantage, right?

Oh, sir, for decades you've scored points at my
Expense, scorned my briefs, denied my lengthy
Motions meant to blow smoke for a client

Late for court, then piled opprobrium
And obloquy, contumely, when you could,
In great gobs on my head, heaped it high

And steaming, stinking bad, and why? Just 'cause
Some man or woman wants his former life
Restored, wants the endless second chance she's

Guaranteed by law, great legs, great loads
Of cash, the flat right, once you'd made a mess
Of marriage, to take another ticket, pick

A partner on the floor, then do the dance
That makes the dream come true, or not. That's it.
But let me show up early on some morning

I've a client due in court, look in
At eight or nine, spend an idle moment
Whittling spit, dropping shucks, making

Small talk with a friend—how's your mother?
How's your father? how's your old wah-zoo?—
Then let that friend—you know the odds against

This sort of thing—turn up presiding
In my client's case, why, land's sakes, sir,
Imagine what they'd say. And people can be

Cruel, cruel as . . . artichokes or arty . . .
Folks or little paper cuts, and if
That's not enough, consider, sir, the mild

Sensation I might've made, retailing things
Heard first among that bunch of legal soaks
Who crowd the Zinc Bar across the street

Or power-lunch in padded booths lining
The dim-lit beanery down the block known locally
As Puds, seems (to give you just

The one example) there's this judge—stuffed
With praise, stiff with pride, sitting since
The late war's close (and no one knows for sure

Which war that was)—abhors divorce, believes
To get through life, we pull our wagon one
Of just two ways: single hitched or yoked

In pairs, and if the latter, parted
Only when death cuts the trace, slaps
A rump, and runs the live one off, seems to think

It's still last century's turn when folks
Expected maybe they'd see forty, maybe
Not, but nothing much beyond, days

Long past when marriage had, let's say, a more
Condensed agenda what with childbirth, lockjaw,
Spanish flu, not to mention, mind you,

Several dozen deadly ordinary
Ills penicillin put an end to,
Whisking people off at will. Well,

In those days when your marriage went to pot,
The best advice you'd get was just sit tight,
Hang on a year or so, maybe four,

Might be five, odds were your wife or you
Would bite the big one long before it came
To that, but now'days, sir, when natural causes

Don't quite pack the wallop they once did and
Folks routinely make it to their eighties, well,
A long, bad marriage is the Chateau d'If,

You don't get out, don't stumble mumbling from
Your cell into the sun until your fingernails
And hair are long as Howard Hughes's, dirty

And deranged—just the sort of endless
Sentence, sir, divorce did away with
Some years back, yet here's this judge, disposing

People's fates on his own say-so, saying no,
Saying folks break up so easily
So often now no one's left

To stand by his sworn word, to shoulder stiff
Commitments, or foot the whopping bill when it
Comes due (presented by a huffy waiter whose

Moist upper lip and eyebrow move
As one). That's why, this same judge claims, our
country's
Much declined from its high point (sometime

Around the end of World War II) when if
We said we'd save somebody's hash, by God
We'd eat that hash for dinner cold in foxholes

Till we did. But oh the times! and oh
The shallow ways now'days!, he'd say (and that's
Just the way he says it too, like Cicero

Berating What's-His-Name?, Cantaloupe,
Catalogue, you know the one I mean),
We've fallen from the high ground that was ours,

Till now we're hardly worth, come Mondays, half
A cup of warm spit, strutting our mean
Egos on a leash, scared of obligations

Made without a chute attached,
Small folk, deeply careless, yet so much
Obsessed with our own looks, we fear bad-hair days

Like the thought of crabs, mutts mostly, unable
To imagine inner lives not ours and with
No heroes left unless, of course, you count

A thousand sordid entertainers. Now . . .
(Here's where this judge I'm quoting always
Pauses for effect, takes a breath,

Sips a drink, pats his forehead with
A napkin till he feels himself restored
Then shouts), which one, speak up, which one of you

Lost souls (did I say "lost"? I meant "mislaid")
Can still construe the sense of "once for all,"
Imagine some deed done, some word said

You can't call back, can't have again to do
No matter how you wring and twist in this
World or the next, and if you understand

That's how life is, that's where it gets its weight,
Why, then, I'd say, shrewd folk might learn from that,
Might draw a truer view of simple conduct,

Shrewd folk, but not you folk. With people ripe
As you, it's way too late to grow a soul,
Why, you can't even make your kids behave,

Let alone, set them an example,
Busy as you are: bent on seeming
Young, pretending to be cool, kowtowing

To these twerps who'll still respond beneath
Their breaths, whatever youthful fashion you affect,
"Hey, dude, scope the geezers," and they'd be right.

Still, as sprouts, they can't say that and not
Expect they won't be beaten into mung,
Though not, of course, by you, since you can't even

Keep kids from contracting through TV
A virus spread by what most tests've shown's
The lowest life-form known to man, I mean

The stand-up comic, a swine whose easy, cynical
Asides, nasal whines, knowing
Ways all combine to cast an air

Of hip complicity where everything
Adult's suspect, where parents' motives, fudged first,
Then knocked flat, turn a Vegas lounge act

Just like that! to biting social comment as in
"Bite me!", while all that's trivial, weak,
That wears a shirker's shirt or coward's coat,

Or just bespeaks a self dead set on never
Growing up is sure to be approved
By yay-hoos who've, like clerks in record stores

(Qualified by nothing but a staring
Self-assurance), no right to an opinion
On anything at all, since what they sell's

A toxic oil spill meant to fill the ears
Of adolescents till their foreheads effloresce
In one big zit, an angry headlight, set

To pop and hurl a hard-packed blackhead like
A bullet halfway 'cross the room, splatting
Those around with pus and blood in token

Of the seething rancor teens today
Are choked with once they clap a pair of
        headphones on.
Well, sir, need I go on? By now

I'm sure you've gathered this tough judge whose views
I've been rehearsing thinks there's nothing to us,
Feels, in fact, we're ruined, wrecked, country

In the toilet, culture in the crapper,
And of all this he takes divorce to be,
At once, the major symptom and the cause,

This deep forswearing, sweeping those we've loved
Or lusted for, thought we loved (then, waking
In the drunk tank, turns out barely liked)

Beneath bad conscience's bald carpet, not
To mention that forswearing, deeper than
The first, in which the self suppresses awkward

Pages from its past, cancels deeds
Of trust, recasts a will, filling blanks
With beaux gestes no one who knew you then,

If pressed, can recollect at all, and in
The act, casting off for good the heart's
Last anchor in the real, much the way

Those snooty dames you meet at parties, standing,
Staring in the mirror of a morning,
Get the news firsthand the crow has landed,

Paling, panic, take their faces in
Their hands for a simple tuck-and-roll,
Stretch it here, splice it there, and for

A year or so, it almost looks like new,
Well, maybe not like new, but leastways worth
The sort of dough this animated taxidermy

Goes for, never thinking Mother
Nature, soft and gentle, slow and droll,
Saves her hammer blows for those who'd fiddle

With the work of time, makes them stand
Before that mirror once again, stupefied
By features stretched so much the give's

Gone south, no pliant skin left lapping that
Forgives, that's when a scalding tear wells in
The eye, trickles down a cheek, grown eerie,

Opalescent, clearly when they wish to God
They'd got their old, earned faces back
Again. Indeed, so strongly does this judge

I'm mostly quoting feel about divorce:
Its repercussions, roots, parallel
Expressions of despair in modern dance

That when these cases come before his court
Most times he slows them to a crawl, which is
To say, inserts an extra step, makes

The litigants appear with their attorneys
In his chambers, then forbids the lawyers
Their accustomed roles, instead of adversaries

Has them act, amici curiae,
As advocates of marriage, seeking ways
This one specific union they'd

Been paid to break might yet be saved by simply
Sitting down together 'round a table,
Spending time—much as it might take

(This judge'll clear his schedule any week
For eyewash of this sort)—just to trace
A battling couple's troubles to their source,

Recovering, if they can, some sense of what
They'd each first found appealing in the other,
Thought best, loved most, then lost in time's

Relentless acid bath, and how, see that's
The question, how the very things they'd most
Admired became with years the irritants

That rubbed them raw as cobs till just the sound
Of one another's voices set their teeth
On edge, had them fingering hard crockery

Anent some insupportable
Retort. But what, sir, takes your breath away's
The way the judge demands the lawyers play

A part in this sad therapeutic farce,
Requires they be constructive, give the gutted
Couple free advice about the trials

Ensuing from divorce: suits for custody,
Child support, moving out
Of state, stuff like that, and then to top

It off, he makes these same attorneys, men
Much married (consequently, used to lots
Of yapping), testify like gospel shouters

In a pew about how youth is short
And passion strong and people change with years,
How quitters never win, how life is long,

A marriage longer still, grim death the longest
One of all, crazy stuff like that,
But from the heart, sharing their emotions,

Showing they know how to listen with
A look as this same judge asks Mrs. Muffy
Merkin, "And when your husband called you that,

"How did that make you feel? Just tell us what
You felt." All this the judge exacts from cruel
Attorneys, makes them do, or else sit through,

And keep their faces ruled. Well, sir! I ask you,
How can words evoke the breaking waves
Of high chagrin, despite, humiliation even,

Mounting to hot anger then
That swept the old Zinc Bar the noon this loony
Judge's latest doings first were bruited,

How, indeed? O for a muse of napalm,
As the poet cries, to paint the flames
In eyes already red from years of dry

Martinis (straight up with a twist) or draw
The great veins standing out in necks,
The throbbing temples shadowed by sharp edges of

Some poorly made or badly placed
Toupee, how conjure lastly, sir, the uproar
And the outrage and the shame (for they

Cried "Shame!") that men of their degree, brother
Lawyers, trained in feint and parry, cut
And thrust, should be constrained to serve as stooges,

Biting on their knuckles, making nice.
I ask, Is there a God in heaven still,
Does justice live, that things like this should be?

Well, Bird, those last two sure are stumpers plain
Enough, and your long anecdote—though on
The whole, quite diverting, making time

Fly by while Fox is out patrolling in
The hall, kicking ass, taking names
(Speaking of which, I thought just now I heard

A body fall)—seems, if I may say so,
Short on plot. After all, what's
The point, where's the problem here? That judges,

Like most men on growing older, having once
Had power, find themselves reluctant to
Retire? Or is it just they hold opinions still

They held first fifty years ago: that marriage
Is a contract not so lightly made
Nor lightly broken, Bird, and what most folks

These days believe they're gaining by divorce
Is something every bit as vain as what
They'd sought when they'd first gotten hitched. And by

The way, the judge you've pictured sounds a lot
Like my old mentor, Justice Amos Cottle,
Not to speak of that procedure (so

Annoying, so amusing in your rendering)
Being rather like the one he pioneered
In which attorneys in divorces

Have to act like human beings helping
Humans in distress, not like sharks
Or wolves, or tigers when a-lashing of their tails.

Indeed, Bird, it's a protocol
Works well enough I use it some myself.
Now, correct me if I'm wrong, but haven't

We a sit-down of this sort scheduled
For today, which couldn't have influenced,
I'd lay odds, the shape of your recital,

Its subtle way of making light of agéd,
Honored jurists holding tight like that!
To their convictions come what may, now could it?

II   Ah, sir, as always, thinking ill, you catch
Me up too quick. Those questions put just now
About God's whereabouts and justice's

Poor health turns out were mostly rhetoric,
Markers of a prologue's end, providing us
With background we might need to this

Smug judge's views, before the big banana
Peel of chance'd launched him into complications such
As cheap French novels thrive on,

Which, if you'll allow, I'll relate:
Seems this highly moral judge's wife
Of forty years was seen last week discreetly

Exiting the office of the city's
Top divorce man. Well, sir, you must know,
This tidbit hit the Zinc Bar like a bombshell.

The scandal sleuths were loose. Men used to tossing
Scraps to private peepers got, before
The week was out, the dirty laundry washed:

Word is, six months ago this judge took on
A clerk, best schools, high grades, quite striking in
Appearance too, or, as they'd toast her at

The Zinc, "Here's to the law clerk with the rack,"
Long hair, long legs, long everything, a feminist
But not averse to wiggling

Her butt, sir, if she thought that that would do her
Any good, you know the type. At any
Rate, they hit it off at once—father-

Daughter stuff, "Oh, sir, you're so wise,"
"Oh, no, Miss Brickhouse, you're a clever pupil,"
Garbage of that sort. And then one day,

Alone together in the judge's chambers,
Checking cases cited in a brief,
She came around his desk, intending only

To point out some precedent she'd found
In that same law book lying open there
Before him, but, in leaning down to mark

The spot, her long blonde hair, by accident
Unfurling, fell across the shoulder of
His coat, grazing neck and cheek and she

Thought sure he'd caught his breath, stiffened in
His chair, so when their glances, swiftly meeting,
Married, bedded, strained, then fell back sweating

Into sleep, she knew the score, she swept
A long arm backwards 'cross the desk to send
The contents flying, farewell Coke and Blackstone,

Kiss the civil and the penal code
Good-bye, along with several ornamental
Pens, a blotter trimmed in leather, one brass

Lamp, his briar pipes, his dog, his cruel
Malacca swagger stick, assorted odds
And ends scattered madly on the floor,

Then she, gazing deep into his eyes,
Grabbed this shaken jurist by the ears and they . . .
Well, as the naval poet Dante

Says somewhere, Once the desk was cleared
For action fore and aft, I dare say they, uh,
Read no more that day in that big book—

That's if you catch his drift, and if you don't,
Who cares? because what started as a burst
Of tender passion turned alas! too soon

To one long string of frenzied nooners on
The rug, until, as often happens, sir,
The injured wife got wind of what was up.

Who knows how? Lipstick on his collar,
Blonde hairs on his coat, a trout in the milk.
As I remember, Mr. Justice Holmes

Is eloquent in U.S. versus Pennsylvania
Coke on how some kinds of circumstantial
Evidence are pretty strong. But there's

The rub, you see—the judge's wife knew law enough
To know she'd never sock him with a
Whopping judgment for divorce by claiming

Hanky-panky with a tootsie (so
Correct had been his reputation up to now
Where women were concerned) unless,

Of course, she had the goods in hand, hard proof,
Preferably the photographic sort—
That's where her plan took root. She knew

At noon he always took a nap—first locked
His office door, then lay down on the couch,
But now she'd guessed he'd varied his routine,

That when the door was locked, someone lay down
On him. Well, as it happened, every day
Twelve sharp, the judge's secretary, lunching

Out, 'd leave the outer office door
Unlocked, the inner office door key loose beneath
The blotter on her desk. Aware

Of this, the judge's wife selects her time,
Makes her way unnoticed four flights up,
Then waits there, hidden, stewing in a stall

Inside the Ladies', till the courthouse clock
Strikes the quarter hour when she hits
The outer door, sir, going sixty, scoops

The key up off the desk and has the inner
Door unlocked and open in one motion,
Rushing blindly in, camera at

The ready, boom! she trips and pitches forward,
Falling flat there on her face, upset,
It seems, by several naked legs. Well, sir,

This judge's wife, God bless her!, had
Quick reflexes and presence under pressure too,
That let her, turning in midair,

Squeeze off a photo as she fell, showing,
So I'm told, the judge, down on all fours,
Wearing nothing but his long black robe

And socks—that's if you fail to count the law
Clerk's panties on his head. Indeed, sir, that
Young woman also figures in the picture:

Lying on her back in what you'd call
The almost all together, striving mightily in one
Motion there to cover with her

Hands at once her face, her breasts, her crotch
And finding that, alack!, she hadn't hands
Enough. No doubt you're wondering how, sir, having

Never seen the photo, I could still
Describe these things—a point well taken. Seems
The lawyer Mrs. Judge retained, in trying

To dispel before the lawsuit got
To court her husband's well-known rep for scrupulous
Behavior with the ladies, showed

Some friends the telltale photo, colleagues mostly,
Five or six, then swore them each to secrecy,
You see. Imagine if you will the scene

Next day at cocktail hour in the old
Zinc Bar when every second patron claimed
To've seen the photograph in question so as

Not to have his fellows think he wasn't
In the loop, though no two versions of
Its contents quite agreed, everything

From "bumping heads al fresco in a closet"
(Mentioned by some soak whose specialty
Was torts. Or maybe tarts?) to "faire la bête

À deux dos sans cesser" (proposed by one
Acquainted with le code Napoléon, no doubt),
And Lord! the tabloid captions they

Came up with, ranging all the way from "Goat
And girlie do the horizontal hula
Without ukes" to "Learned jurist snapped

While poring over law clerk's briefs," then topping that
With "Corpulent corpus delicti, caught in
Flagrante delicto, doing delicious delovely!"

Well, let me tell you now, that afternoon
The old Zinc Bar outdid itself, its clientele
Exhibiting for any skeptics in

The group the plain untruth of that old Chinese
Adage, for, sir, in a dim-lit barroom's
Smoky haze, who could rightly say

A thousand bandied words weren't worth way more
Than one poor randy picture? Still, don't get
The wrong idea. Though my version of

The photo's contents came from jawing in
The bar that afternoon, my sources were
Impeccable: I heard it from a man,

Who heard it from a girl, who heard it from
The Prince of Wales—just like in the song.
Yet, sir, weighing all the facts, shouldn't we

Condemn the lack of ethics shown by Mrs.
Judge's lawyer, playing tricks to snag
A verdict in the court of common gossip?

Clearly, sir, I think we must. I think
In fact his name should be inscribed in India
Ink in some big book, then have a line

Struck through it, showing disapproval. So,
With that in mind, I tried to get his name,
But none of those who claimed to've seen the photo

Knew a thing about it (well, you see
The shrewdness of his play: floating
Killer info through his agents in

A crowd of soused attorneys so he couldn't
Be connected with the show, like pouring
Poison in a water hole by night),

But did I let this Moriarty's subtleties
Deter me? Not a minute, no,
I pumped as many patrons downing shooters

At the bar there as I dared without
Arousing their suspicions, asking, Did
They catch the source of this convenient rumor,

Know the guy who'd shown the photo? Nothing,
Not a word, not till some fellow, sidling up,
Took the barstool next to mine,

Saying how he'd heard I was looking
For a man, funny little fellow,
Scar here on his cheek, cut right through

The lip, talked with a lisp. Next thing I know
He's tipping me the wink, lays a finger
On his nose, then starts to say the name

He thinks I'm after, sir, when all at once
A roar, erupting from the crowd, blots it out,
Name that sounds like Box or Socks, near

As I can tell through all the noise, because,
You see, the TV's on above the bar
Where someone's sunk a putt, scored a goal,

Got a hit, or what?, I don't know,
I turned, trying to make out the cause
But must've missed it, then when I turned back,

The little guy was gone. Though, come to think now,
Maybe what he said was, How'd I like
To see him in his boxer shorts and socks?,

That's when the roar went up, the guy got scared
And ran away, because you know, the Zinc's
Never been that kind of bar, too full

Of micks who, once they get a snootful, look
To play some whack-a-daisy without needing
Much excuse. At any rate, I never got

The name, never saw the little guy
Again, never won the Nobel Prize for peace.
And since that's all I know, I think I'll stop.

Now wait a minute, Bird. Let me get
This straight, you mean the moral of this monumental
Tale is nothing more than judges

Get divorced, doctors catch the clap,
Hangmen also die, is that the point?
'Cause if it is and you've been using up

My time for that, I think you should be trampled
Under foot, indeed, I've half a mind
To step around my desk and trample you

Myself except I know there's lots more to
This story that's unsaid. Now, for instance,
This attorney you end up with almost

As an afterthought—strikes me, Bird, he's
The tale's real point, indeed, seems like a sort
Both of us might know, and though you're sure

You never got his name, might turn out he's
A lawyer you'd crossed swords with more than once,
Who'd kicked your butt around the block. And now,

What's this? Can it be? Yes, it is—
The fellow tries to win by leaking info
In a case, demeaning stuff (real or rumored)

That impugns a reputation,
Stuff that gives a lawyer extra lev'rage
If his client means to force a

Settlement outright before the matter goes to
Court. And who's the chump whose reputation
Gets laid waste? Why, Bird, a judge, of course.

And who's the type most like to care? Why,
Let me see? Could it be another
Judge, who feels, "If this young man thinks judges

Are his meat, here's one porkchop's going
To bite his ass off chomp! first chance he gets"?
Makes sense—a senior jurist who, though unacquainted

With the parties in the case,
Feels the brotherhood of judges, not
To say, the pride of jurisprudence, might

Require henceforth this sly attorney's every
Motion, strong objection be dismissed
Or overruled. Indeed, a lawyer leaking

Rumors meant to sink a judge, who finds
Himself tripped up in turn, Bird, by some legal
Squit retailing gossip to a jurist

"Just in passing" has a sort of fatal
Symmetry, suggesting rough justice.
Satisfying? . . . Certainly—that's if

There's any truth in what you've said—which I
Don't know, though I can guess. So, Bird, before
Retirement intervenes, just see who's at

The door there, will you? I thought I heard a knock,
Could be Fox. Ah, yes . . . Good Lord! What happened,
Fox? Your hair looks like it flew the red-eye

From the coast, and your school tie, it's all
Askew, pulled so tight your eyes are bulging.
Lord, I'd say someone'd jumped you from

Behind, then tried to turn your head around
Full circle, Fox, by yanking on a collar wing,
Yet only managed, since I'm sure you fought back well

Before you ran, to tear it halfway
Off, then left it hanging down your back,
But, Fox, come in, come in, sit down, sit down.

Thank you, sir. Could I have a drink
Of water, please? You won't believe what I've
Been through. Oh, thanks . . . that hit the spot.
    Well, judge,

I've had the kind of time outside just now
That, if I told you what had happened,
Told you half, you'd call me, sir, a liar.

No, Mr. Fox, not even if I thought it.
But take a breath, compose yourself. Now start
Again. Good Lord! you look just like hell's bunghole.

Well, that's what I've been through. Recall that when
I stepped out in the hall to find the cause
Of that persistent racket interrupting

Our exchange, you authorized, indeed,
I might say, deputized me, sir, to quell
Whatever ruckus'd been let loose among

The folk. Well now, first thing I see's this group,
They're milling 'round a man down on one knee,
Can't see his face, the crowd's too thick, and so I

Ask a stander by, What hath occurred?,
You know the drill. Fellow says, Damnedest
Thing I ever saw!, there's this couple, see's,

Been waiting in the hall here for
A while, 'specting they'd be called any
Time, 's why they're walking back and forth,

Up and down, and every time they pass, hello!,
They zing each other with another
Word until at last the guy's so mad

He stops and starts to read the riot act,
Going at it with a will, and then some.
Well now, I don't get every word because

The mug's emoting in a fierce whisper, see,
But what I do get sounds like this:
"Blah-de-blah-de-blah thick ankles, yah-

De-yah-de-yah fat thighs, la-de-da-
De-da lard ass," well, now, that's just about
The time this gal thinks, Whoa! gettin' kinda

Personal, ain't it, Slick? So what's the dame's
Reply? Quick as death she steps inside
His left, plants her feet, then shoots a straight

Right hand with all she's got (thighs, ass, and massive
Ankles thrown behind it), catching him
Right here above the heart so hard his gaze

Gets goofy, staggering back a step or two,
Then makes his big mistake, see, starts
Coming toward her, could be it's a reflex,

Could be for a moment he goes crazy 'cause the
Gal's already moving with
Her left, 's got this pocket book, looks like

A small valise filled with bricks, swinging
By a strap slung low, heading forward so it
Gets him where he parties, right

In the ol' "gagoonies" like the beaners say.
Eyes go blank, face goes gray, mouth
Goes "Oof!", next thing I know he's grabbed his groin

Two-handed, seeing can he stop that breathless
Ringing in his stones by sucking wind
Before he crumples forward on one knee,

Big beads of sweat standing on his forehead.
Well, you think this dame was done? Not yet,
Not even started. Seems like sometime, somewhere,

Someone'd shown her how you throw a left hook off
A jab. (Matter of fact, first time
I saw this dolly's face I thought, This one's

Done some dancing in the ring, 's been
Tagged plenty too.) At any rate,
She shortens up the strap, swings the purse again,

Roundhouse fashion with her left, and
Catches him real good, right here in the
Temple, kind of blow the thudding sound

Of which makes people standing 'round a little sick,
That's when the guy throws in the other
Knee. So lookit, got the shot? He's kneeling

In the hall, both hands on his crotch,
Bent a little forward now as she
Steps up, grabs a handful of his hair

Either side like it's a loving cup,
Then kicks him in the stomach, not some sideways,
Sissy kick like a Chinaman

Or Jap but like a teenage tomboy playing
Football with her brothers' friends who's dropping
Back to punt while being rushed and sees

She's got to get the kick off fast before a
Bunch of sweaty boys, breaking through,
Gang-tackle her and in the writhing pileup

Cop a feel—that's what the kick was like.
And trust me, mac, if some bystander hadn't
Pushed himself between the two when she

Drew back her right fist for a nasty upper cut,
I think it would have killed him, yes,
Felled him right there on the spot. Never

Saw a thing to beat it, no. Damnedest
Thing I ever saw! Well, sir, that's what
The fellow had to say, hat pushed back,

Brim turned up, toothpick in his mouth,
Cigarette behind his ear, looked like
A race-track tout, though prob'bly nothing more

Than some bail bondsman's seedy gofer, still,
His blow-by-blow recital made me see it
Just as if I'd been there. Moreover, in

The time it took to tell, the crowd around
The man down on the floor had thinned and then
Imagine my surprise, no, make that my

Chagrin, on finding that this erstwhile human
Punching bag, now doubled up before
Me there, who'd been the burden of the ferret's

Tale, was my old friend and client Mr. Fish.
Picture my embarrassment. Well, of course,
I went to his assistance, knelt to help,

Amazed the way he held himself together,
Both hands squeezing tight, gulping air
In awful mouthfuls, looking, sir, for all

The world like some enormous goldfish out
Of water, seeing could he suck in one
Great breath his aching eyeballs back into

Their sockets. I said, "Bill Fish, old friend,
    what's happened?
Won't you speak?" because, sir, all he'd managed
To get out was "ech-ech-ech-ech-ech,"

While beckoning me nearer with his head,
As if he'd some breathtaking secret to impart,
But as he raised his eyes up, sir,

A look of such fear fell across his face
It could have been a shadow cast by some
Impending object, making him gasp out

In one convulsive whisper, "Gonads! It's
Kid Fister! Bathe yourself!" though clearly, sir,
In retrospect the words he said were, "Good God!

It's the sister! Save yourself!" because
At once, as if a wildcat jumped me from behind,
My ear was grabbed on one side, collar

Wing grasped tightly on the other just
As someone hissed, "Yes, and you're another,
You worthless turkey buzzard!" punctuating

Each harsh syllable with a shake so hard,
Had my teeth not been my own, sir, if,
For instance, I'd a wobbly upper plate

Like Mr. Bird, I couldn't've guaranteed just then
They wouldn't've gone shooting out
My mouth and struck poor frightened Fish right on

The conk. Meanwhile, whatever fiend from hell
Had me from behind, she shook and hissed
Relentlessly, saying things I wouldn't

Dare repeat, let alone try to spell,
Things like "You dirty rack-a-fratch!
You thimblerigging bumblepuppy!" What's that?

I don't know what that even means. I felt
Just like a rag doll snatched up by some moron,
Yanked up bodily knees to feet

By ear and collar wing, then forced back down
Again, up and down, up and down,
Dunked, sir, like a doughnut, wrung out like some

Union suit that's wet, then stretched and ratcheted
Across a washboard till, abrupt as it
Began, it stopped, I'd been cut loose, cast off

In tatters, left to settle limply toward
The floor while watching Fish's face through half-shut
Eyes, seeing if that look of fear had gone,

If I dared turn my head to see. Well, sir,
In short, it had, I did, but who or what'd
Hit me stayed a myst'ry still, since they'd quick

Beat it down the hall and 'round the corner,
Though my old friend Fish had seen, knew
The culprit, so, sir, turning back in time

To catch him as he stumbled to his feet,
Pale and on the point of fainting, as
I asked, he gasped, "A Kansas twister! Moose

Or mouse? A brick or bat? What can it matter!"
Well, sir, I must admit, by this point I'd had
Just about enough. I grasped Fish by

The shoulders, shook him like a vodka Gibson,
Much as I'd myself been shaken, shouted out,
"God damn it, Fish, make sense!" when he

Collapsed and in a nonce soprano fairly
Crooned, "My wife's big sister! Huge as a house!
Quick as a cat! Mad as a hatter!" Well, that,

At least, got cleared up. So, when Fish regaining
Strength began to tell me what'd happened,
How he'd shown up early, looking for

Your chambers, set to meet with you
And me, his wife and her attorney, face to face,
Making one last effort toward

A reconciliation much as you'd
Yourself requested, what's he find except
The wife is late and in her place the large,

Unstable, wholly evil sister's shown up,
Bent on giving her sad sibling such
Emotional support as she was able,

Albeit oiled and spoiling for a fight.
Now remind me, did I mention Fish
And this big sister'd never liked each other

Much? I didn't? Well, . . . you bet! Consequently,
Dirty looks between the two
Went back and forth, these led to words, and words

In turn led, sir, to what they're often said to.
As the fellow with the ferret face
So aptly phrased it: "How about a mug

That likes to run his mouth, locating in
A state without a standing eight-count, huh?
Go figure that one out." Well, sir, I'd heard

Enough. At once I tried to rally Fish's
Spirits since, as he'd recounted these events,
His eyes'd got a look I didn't like,

That thousand-yard gaze you see in grunts
When rifle companies, kept too long in action,
First get pulled out of the line for R and R.

You know, sir, on a personal note,
Years back when Fish and I first met, he'd just
Been separated from the Corps, as I'd

Been from the Navy, so, with that in mind,
I tried a trick, moving 'round behind him
As he tottered there in place, I shouted out,

"Lance-Corporal Fish, atten-hut!" Well, he seemed
To snap to in an instant with me barking,
"Brace your shoulders, suck your gut, thumbs

Along your seams!" Indeed, it seemed to stiffen
His resolve, so I continued, "Listen up,
You jarhead!" (just imagine the effect, sir,

When a sailor calls them that—
Talk about commanding their attention)
"Soon, Fish, you'll be in before the judge,

"Stand up straight, eyes front, answer
When addressed. And be a man. No acting
Like a wuss because some girl who wants

"To be a truck, yanked your hair, hauled off
And kicked you in the gut. Leave her to me.
Big as she is, she can't get far unnoticed.

"Meanwhile, you just stay here, man your post,
Keep a look out. If the enemy
Returns, don't attempt to re-engage,

"Instead, fall back, keeping contact. Meantime,
Once I've rounded up fresh troops, I'll head
This way, make a quick reconnaissance

"In force, seal the flanks, seek the first
Terrain favoring surprise, then close
Before we lose the light." (That military

Lingo, sir, God help me but I do
Love it so.) That's when I left Fish there
And started looking for a bailiff,

The large black man, I think his name is Biggs,
Found him, then together we went searching
For the sister, turned a corner, there

She was, far end of the hallway, touching
Up her makeup with a mortar board
And trowel. Well, sir, Biggs took one long good look,

Turned to me and said, "Mr. Fox,
Wait here, till I see can I get Dobbs
To back me up." You know Dobbs, sir, short,

Built like a cannon ball, well now, quick
As that! here they both come back, striding
Past me down the hall, and Biggs, turning,

Winks at me and says, "Check your razors,
Check your guns, we gonna be wrestlin'
When de wagon comes!" And, sure enough, another
minute

Three of them were rolling on the floor,
Biggs and Dobbs and great big sister, locked
In various choke holds, and let tell you, sir,

This gal was winning! Biggs'd got his arm around
Her neck, pulling from behind, the same
Way she had Dobbs, then she rolled backwards flat

On Biggs's chest, taking Dobbs right with her,
That's when Biggs's breathing fell apart,
Followed quick by Dobbs's speech, his windpipe

Wedged within the crook of sis's elbow,
Trying to shout numbers in
A handheld walkie-talkie, signifying,

So I gather, "Officer down, needs
Assistance." Well, sir, what had started as
A simple apprehension for assault,

Before my eyes, became the main event.
The hour was late, and I thought sure by now
Fish's wife had come, that you'd be waiting

For me in your chambers, set to start
Proceedings, so I left them there (the issue
Still in doubt), though vowing like MacArthur

I'd return. Well now, I'm happy to
Report, while coming back, two bailiffs passed me
In the opposite direction on

The run, heading for the noise, much
As Blucher, marching toward the sound
Of cannon, came in time to whip the French.

And, sir, if you'll allow me here the one
Observation, well, I thought how bailiffs
Mostly are unsung, these little folk

Whose lives, often empty and banal,
Are sacrificed for us with real abandon
When there's trouble in the building. That's

The reason, when these brave men make it back,
They deserve some note be taken. I
Particularly commend our Mr. Biggs,

For brio in the face of sure humiliation,
Followed closely, sir, by Mr.
Dobbs, for having such a neck this gal

Could pull all day and not dislodge his head.
Both men've earned a medal, bit of ribbon,
At least a strong notation in their jackets.

I see. . . . No, I don't. Why did I say that?
I think it's the effect, Fox, born of having
Bird go on about some judge's indiscretions

Till he ends up with the thought we two,
Can you believe it?, ought formally inscribe
The judge's wife's attorney's name in some

Big book, then strike a line right through it. That's
When you came stumbling in, Fox, fresh from foreign
Wars, making like some dustup in the hall's

The second wave ashore at D-day,
Bent on having me out decorating
Bailiffs. Well, what's next? Nothing in

My horoscope this morning in the paper
Gave a hint, the slightest mention how
The day might take a turn and run away,

But then I should've known, once I saw
This case included on the docket, knew
You two would be appearing for the parties

With your lengthy rivalry as freight
Complicating things, a rivalry
Beginning with/including (some say one,

Some the other) Fox's rumored "candle-stein"
Affair (as if they'd only met
In dim-lit bistros built in cellars) with the

First Mrs. Bird. Yes, I really
Should've known. But let me warn you both,
That baggage stays outside. We're here to help

Two people having problems, understood?
No scoring points, no cheap shots—act like gentlemen
Who, although the woe in marriage pays

For your Italian suits, are still compassionate
Enough to make your wide experience
Of life, of people going through

Domestic meltdown, useful in dispelling
Misconceptions, building bridges, finding
Compromises leading to the hope

These folks might not go postal over breakfast
If they stuck it out some more, and if,
When all is said, love and trust

Are lost beyond recovery, then we bring
It to an end, with dignity and fairness
All around. That's all I ask, and what

I mean to have. And speaking of compassion,
No offense intended, Fox, in summarizing
With such brusqueness what'd happened

In the hall just now, then blowing off
Your feeling footnote on the bailiffs. Indeed,
No man, no group of men, should have to suffer

What the three of you went through, let alone
Officers of the court pursuing
Noise abatement. Still, Fox, as I always

Say, look on the brighter side. You're
Recently divorced (what is it? number
Four, number five), prob'bly back out

Trying to hit on chicks and here's a chick
Ups and hits on you. Well, let me tell you, Fox,
It's been my observation through

The years, close up and at a distance, the really
Hot ones like it rough, and now you two
Are well beyond the stage of needing introductions.

III

Ah, sir, I know how much you love
Your little jokes, but this gal was a killer.
Still, supposing there's some truth in what

You've said about the hot ones, how they like it
With the bark on, and, supposing more,
That observation holds, sir, in reverse, then I'd say,

Judging by her grip, this dame
Must be a scorcher in the sack, but when
It comes to that, who am I to judge?

'Cause me and women, well . . . you know, I married
Five but never got the sense of what
They wanted, which is to say, never thought

They knew themselves. Oh, sure, they're charming
Creatures mostly. Why, sir, I remember one who'd
Wait for me at home when she came in

From playing three quick sets of tennis, cropped
Blonde hair still moist, her upper lip
Still glistening with sweat, wait curled up on a long

Black leather couch wearing nothing but
A damp T-shirt and rolltop cotton socks,
Looking as she lay, sir, like a tasty

Little lamb chop—that's when she'd grin, begin
To growl down low, crawling on all fours
Across the room to where I sat, flicking

Carelessly about me with my braided
Leather crop, smoking a cigar,
Bored yet watching closely as she rubbed

Her sweat-flushed cheek, her close-cropped head
    against
The polished uppers of my English riding
Boots, then stuck her tongue out, starting in

To lick in length'ning strokes the boots from toe
To shank, growling all the while, until I'd grab
A handful of blonde hair, cruelly

Twisting it to bring her head up as I
Whispered that, like Murdstone, I'd soon make her
Wince and whimper, ran the crop along

Her cheek, down her slowly pulsing throat,
Along her shoulder, then across her heaving
Shirt front where it outlined two large mounds

Of ripening pleasure, slowly lifted one
To flick its stiffening tip, then let it drop,
That's when, leaning down, I'd breathe into

Her ear, "You're a wicked little animal
Who needs stiff discipline," then quick as that!
I'd twist her hair, turning the little minx

Around there on all fours, sir, with a yelp
To snick her smartly with my crop across
Trim buttocks, taut and writhing, till she purred,

Then meekly turned her head, begging "Mr. Man"
With liquid eyes, "Oh, sir, oh please . . . " for private
Riding lessons on the floor, that's when . . .

That's when!?—my God, Fox, that's enough! We've learned
Much more about your private life's alarming
Predilections than we'd ever cared

To know, or come to know from years of mere
Professional association, so
I'm warning you now, Fox, had this last

Salacious revelation taken place
With ladies present—Mrs. Fish, for instance,
Even that ball-busting sister—why, sir,

I'd've had to call the bailiff, have him place you
In restraints, maybe gag you if
These twisted recollections still persisted,

Though, Fox, given what you've said, I'm not
So sure you wouldn't've liked that, liked that quite
A bit, God help you, bo'. But get this straight,

While agreeing with your first remark
About the charms of women, I object
To your implicit denigration of

The big ones. Why, Fox, you see before you one
Who's spent a lifetime loving large women, yes,
And never thought my time was wasted, no,

'Cause anyone can tell you, had
You ever cared to ask, they're firm to pinch,
Fun to hug, and when you grab a handful

Of 'em, both hands come back full, Fox, as the
Swifties used to say when I was young.
Indeed, boys, I especially liked the ones

Who moaned and screamed, then told the sweetest lies
In bed, the ones who'd urge you on to greater
Depths by alternating dovelike, fluted oo-ings

With high strident cries of urgent need,
Thrusting all the while their stockinged
Legs up in the air so straight they'd stretch

The filmy mesh, black and tight, across
Those round hard heels, then swing them down to catch you
Snug beneath the buns and pull you straight up in . . .

"To paradise," dragging nails
Across your back and panting, "Ray, oh Ray,
You're the man, you're the one, oh, Ray,

"Give it to me, baby, you're the biggest,
You're the greatest, God! go deeper, Ray,
Harder, Ray, faster, Ray, now, Ray,

"Yes, Ray, oh, Ray, now, now! OOOH RAAAY!
You're the best"—in those days, boys, I went
By the name of Ray, which needn't much concern you

Here unless you'd thought that, given I'd
A different name now, maybe these Homeric
Deeds were feats done by some other guy

Overheard while standing on a chair
Below a transom opened up between
Adjoining rooms renting by the hour

In some cheap seaside hotel. No, no,
I'm the guy, le gros baton c'est moi,
If I do say so myself. But, Bird,

It's not like you to be so silent for
So long. You look like you've been sucking on a lemon.
What's the matter? Spit it out.

Sir, I'm shocked, shocked to find that conversations
Of this sort—sexist, prejudicial,
Not to say, arousing—still

Take place inside a judge's chambers after
Years of case law nailing just such bawdy
Stories in the workplace, shocked because,

As Mrs. Fish's lawyer, sir, I stand
In loco feminae, as it were, enduring
Much the same humiliation she'd've

Felt had she been party to this ribald,
Raucous mimicry of female cries
Emitted during coitus or, sir, Fox's

Fantasies that he's that French marquis
Who whacked girls' heinies with a switch—his name
Escapes me at the moment but I'm sure

You know the marquis I've in mind. Indeed,
I trust, sir, I'm no priss, no prude, no sis.
I've been around, I know the score. What's more,

JOHN
BRICUTH

56

I've been around a few I scored myself,
Everything from ladies of the evening
Leaning up against a lamppost greeting you with

"Hello, sailor!" in Marseilles to
Dolls of indeterminate age who nurse
Exotic drinks, exotic hopes late afternoons

In dim-lit cocktail lounges, languid there
In black spaghetti-strapped, come-and-get-me
Dresses cut so low in front

Their wallys wipe the bar while waiting for
The sort of legal lions that stalk these water holes
At dusk, looking to pick off a

Dazed stray, maybe bag an aging straggler.
Yes, I've known them all already, known them all
(Though not the kind of knowing Prufrock

Meant, no, no, much more like what the Bible
Had in mind), from pert cheerleaders panting
In the backseat of my car when I

Turned seventeen (talk about the ones
Who'd cheer you on), why, I remember once
These three gymnastic red-hots, blonde and bulging in

Their matching letter sweaters, short
Accordion-pleated skirts, and scuffed-up saddle
Shoes, had squeezed their sweet bods tight

Into the front seat of my beat-up Chevy coming
Back from some big game when, of a sudden
On a dare, I turned off there and parked

And these three cookies piled in back, where one
Pulled off her sweater, swung it 'round her head,
And yelled, "Hey, gang! Let's do a locomotive just

For Birdy!" Well, sir, as you know, the term
Refers to cheers requiring pistonlike,
Repetitive enunciation reminiscent

Of a railroad engine entering
A tunnel, though, to tell the truth,
Judging by their moves, I'd guessed that they'd

A different pistonlike, repeated, local
Motion then in mind, your honor,
If you take my point. Ah yes, I've known them all

Already, known them all—from those fond
      teenage years
Right down, sir, to the middle of
Last week when I was dancing with a colleague's

Wife after dinner at the country club
(The firm's annual dinner dance it was),
Having noticed all that evening she'd been

Giving me the eye, rubbing up
Against me at the table, hand along
My sleeve to get my full attention when

She talked, you know the signs, and so, asking
Her to dance, I thought I'd try a little
Test I have to see if gals who flirt

Mean business, mean to put out when their dinner's
     paid for,
Not just tease, as some do, trying
To stir things up as proof they're still attractive,

Maybe make their husbands jealous, start a
Fist fight in a night club, that's why as we
Danced, quite suddenly I slid my hand

From where it rested, middle of her shoulder blades,
Right down her spine as if I meant
To grab a luscious bun and squeeze it like

A grapefruit, stopping short, sir, at that juncture
Where the backbone meets the butt, then pressing
Firmly with three fingers there while leaning

Close to breathe warm words within her whorléd
Ear, "I love your breasts, I'd love to smear them
Thick with honey, then take the whole night long

To lick them clean." That's when, providing, sir,
She hasn't slapped your face off, should
Your fingertips detect the slightest soupçon

Of a frisson in that region just
Adjacent to her bum, you'll know you've got
A keeper, much as I did with my colleague's wife,

Filing her instinctive tremor on
The dance floor in that mental Rolodex
Of chicks I keep against gray rainy days when

One gets bored, wants a drink or two,
A laugh, a smile, a chance to get your rocket
Polished absent any obligation,

Yes, I've known them all already, known
Them all. That's why I must object to these
Insensitive, demeaning anecdotes

Such as you and Fox indulge in, making
Women seem inert pneumatic objects
Only fit to gratify arrested

Adolescent lust, indeed, object
With every fiber of my being, seeing
That I stand before you here the legally

Constituted simulacrum of Mrs.
Fish, who'd surely have resented your remarks—
If gals showed up for things on time.

Now let me get this straight, Bird, you're objecting,
Crazy as it seems, to comments made
By Fox and me regarding members of

The fairer sex with whom we'd shared a tender
Moment (though as I recall in Fox's
Case the moment seemed more kinky than

Consensual, yes), objecting, Bird, on grounds
These little reminiscences of ours
Were sexist, prejudicial, plain insensitive

To women's feelings, never recognizing once
The need to reconcile
Such charges with your own hormonal strolls

Down mem'ry lane accompanied by streetwalkers,
Lounge lurkers, cheerleaders, not to mention some
Poor colleague's tipsy, tasteless wife, never

Conscious once, Bird, of the beam in your
Own eye. And you object? Object to what?
Your bird-shot logic makes no sense at all!

No, sir! And it never will. You see,
I've got the big advantage of you here,
Being well acquainted with Bird's ways

From years of butting heads, his manners, leaps
Of logic, general background (since I've actually
Seen his résumé). Did you know

Our Mr. Bird, sir, got his law degree
By correspondence? Yes, indeed, got it
From a law school housed in someone's empty

Basement, situated, so I'm told by
Dicks I hired, in greater (don't you love it?)
Lompoc, California. Next, according

To his vita, he shows up, sir, clerking
Several years for one Judge Crater in
An undisclosed location, leaves to join

The firm of Howard, Howard, and Fine, moving next
To Dewey, Cheatham, and Howe where he
Makes partner. Now the word around the Zinc is

He's about to move again, yes, seems
Our Mr. Bird's just struck a deal with one
Algonquin J. Calhoun, the noted civil

Rights attorney, forming their own firm
That's called, get this, Victims More or Less,
Limited to representing women,

Blacks, Hispanics, Asians, sad white guys
Over sixty-five, and homeless folk—
The sort acquainted with the art of

Falling flat in front of city buses
Just about to stop. Rumor has it
Any day the firm's first TV ads

Begin to air on local stations, using
As their hook a catchy jingle, goes
Like this: "There's no gal who's not our pal,

There's no race that we won't chase, there's
No geezer we don't please, no MTA
That we can't squeeze." Well, sir, I think that song

Conveys the sense of what we're up against
When Mr. Bird is on the case, but what
I don't quite get is what he said at first,

About his standing in for loco fems.
So who's he representing—Mrs. Fish
Or that Tasmanian devil of a sister?

Clearly after what, sir, Biggs and Dobbs
And I went through, I mean to prosecute that
Buster once they clap the bracelets on her.

Yes, Mr. Fox, but not this afternoon,
This afternoon we three have other fish
To fry, so to speak, and your unfortunate

Encounter with the sister forms
No part of this proceeding, nor, Fox, should such
Extramural matters cloud your handling

Of the case, affect the courtesy
Owed to Mrs. Fish or reinflame
An animus against the lady's lawyer.

You tell him, judge! And warn him too
About that sad pastiche of lies, half-truths,
And half-baked innuendoes he cooked up concerning

My career. Why, Fox can't even
Get the jingle right, and when it comes
To alma maters mine has never been

In Lompoc, it's in Lodi! Also, kindly
Tell the gentleman those anecdotes
Regarding pliant women in my past

Were meant as indications I'm no Goody
Two-Shoes when it comes to dames, having
Been as crude and coarse for years as both

Of you and thus, that when my consciousness
Was raised, when I realized the way
I'd always dumped on chicks for fun, I had

To get it off my chest, much as your
Repentant sinner needs to make a full
Confession authorizing, nay, empowering him

To preach to those as lost as he,
And that, sir, in a nutshell was the point
Of those few anecdotes I told, trying

To make Br'er Fox here see the light, maybe
Change his ways with women, cast aside
Both beam and mote before the devil dragged

Him under, sir, by the sharp lapels of his checkered
Coat. That's all my anecdotes intended.
Kindly tell the learned gentleman so.

No, Mr. Bird, I rather think I won't,
Seeing Fox is standing there beside you,
Biting on his thumb. But speaking, Bird,

Of hearing things, I thought I heard
Just now a rapping, as of someone faintly
Tapping, tapping at my chamber door,

Only this and nothing more, so, Fox,
Just see who's at the door there, will you? Could be
It's the Fishes, but if it's instead

Some pompous, talking blackbird rapping for
Admittance, slam the door right in the mucker's
Face, one talking bird a day in here's

Enough 'sfar as I'm concerned. . . . Ah, yes!
Come in, come in. Mr. and Mrs. Fish
I presume. How do you do? Please,

Sit down. You know, of course, your own attorneys.
Mrs. Fish, this is Mr. Fox,
Acting for your husband. Mr. Fish,

This is Mr. Bird who represents
The Mrs. Both your lawyers, doubtless, briefed you
On the purpose of this meeting, still,

I might say just a word before we start.
Seems to me an hour, maybe hour
And a half, wouldn't be too much to ask,

Trying to save a marriage that's survived . . .
Let's see, it's in these papers somewhere . . . yes,
That's lasted twenty-seven years, a lot

Of time, I'd say, to toss away like gum.
That's why we're here. Now I've instructed both
Attorneys they're forbidden any sort

Of adversarial stance in these proceedings,
Only comments from the heart will be
Permitted, caring comments meant to help

The couple reconcile at this late date
If there's a chance, and if there's not, the suit
Goes straight to trial. Yet even in that case

Sit-downs such as these can serve a purpose,
Giving both the parties, as they say on TV
When a jet explodes or gunfire

Rakes the schoolyard, "closure." After all,
If two people call it quits, having
Spent the better part of life locked

In holy headlocks, baggage needs to be
Unpacked, because, you know, your married couples
Grow so much alike in time, sharing

Tastes, swapping habits, starting next
To look alike, then like their pets—that if
They break up hating one another's guts,

Chances are they'll go through life regretting,
If not loathing, something deep inside
Themselves, but more than that, there's the problem,

Once they split, how to deal with, what
To feel about, some twenty, thirty years
Compacted, sacked, and thrown out with a spouse.

Make no mistake, mem'ry's not some slate
You wipe clean with a sponge. Its pictures, sounds,
Bare feel, get ground in deep, and if there're years

Of these jumbled in the wreck, then seems
To me you've got to make some hard decisions,
Tell yourself what part the lengthy passages

Scratched out still play in that self-serving
(Should I say "that self-conserving"?) narrative
We each concoct about, and sometimes

Out of, our own lives, since if you simply
Write years off as waste, don't make at least
Some effort to reclaim them so they'll figure in

Life's overall trajectory
As your great fated interlude, grave test,
Needed detour, not to be refused

If you'd come to that place you'd always known
Was yours . . . well, you see now what I mean, the way
A young knight-errant, wandering years

In stony places looking for the Castle
Marvelous, through forests dark and huge,
Past crags, past overhanging outcrops green

With moss where mountain streams come tumbling
From a height, will stop one day at dusk
In freezing rain, bone-tired, armor rusted,

Limbs grown stiff from sleeping on the ground,
Dismount before a simple peasant's hut,
Find a friendly welcome, food prepared,

A pallet spread before the fire, and as he
Falls asleep there, start to feel he's seen
This place before. Can it be? This hut

The very one where years ago he'd rested on
The first night of his quest? And with
A heavy heart knows the truth, understands

He's journeyed in a circle, hopeless,
Sleeps, and in a dream (some versions have
A dream, some a vision) sees the Castle

Marvelous, that chivalrous ideal
Of welcome, warmth, and nurture's nothing more
Than this same peasant's hut, a thing he'd never've

Recognized years back when first he'd stumbled
On it, not till life had tricked and tried him,
Then returned him to this spot, the place

Unchanged but he changed wholly. Well now, I don't
Say it has to be elaborate as
All that, this tale you tell yourself transforming

Dead ends into detours, still it's got
To be redemptive—and believed. Otherwise
You'll carry those lost years like unpaid freight,

And I'd say, folks, no way you won't end up
Embittered—that or worse, forever blaming
Someone else about the way your case

Turned out, going back and forth like some
Sad sephardic cantor always chanting
"The Spaniard That Blighted My Life—Olé! Oy vey!"

Won't do. We're men and women of the world here,
Don'tcha know? Got the stuff they call
Panache, wear soft hats at rakish angles,

"Easy come, easy go," so what
I say is when it comes to breaking up,
Take the path of debonair, de

Rigueur bon ton, saying with the famous
Female poet Mr. Bird persists
In calling Edna St. Louis Missouri, "After

All, my erstwhile dear, my no longer
Cherished, need we say it was not love,
Just because it perished?" Now that's the line

You take, that's the pose to strike, get done
And then get on with it, and understand
I don't pretend our meeting here today

Can do all that if splitting up's the course
Your hearts are set on, but I do say it's
A start towards getting shut of one another

In the least destructive way. Now by
Tradition the person who speaks first in these
Proceedings is the one who brought the suit.

That's you, Mrs. Fish. So don't be nervous,
Tell us what you feel, how it came
To this, and if there's hope it might be saved.

Remember both these lawyers and myself
Have been divorced, know the pain involved,
And simply mean to help. So, Mrs. Fish?

IV

Let me first apologize, your honor,
Being late and keeping you four waiting.
I'd allowed, I'd thought, lots of time to

Drive, but when I went to start the car,
The darned thing wouldn't start! That's the stuff
Bill always handled, knew about—machines,

Electricity, plumbing, things I've had
To learn from scratch this year since splitting up
But never had the knack for. Well, at any

Rate, when I went back inside to call
A cab, the phone was dead. The storm last night
Dropped a branch across the alley, must've

Got the line, so nothing to do then
But wait around till Marge next door came back
From grocery shopping, judge, and ran me downtown

In the car, that's why I'm late and, as
I say, I do apologize. Also,
As I understand from Bill just now,

Additional apologies are due
To him and Mr. Fox, and maybe to
You too, sir, for the way my sister Gert

Cut up outside a while ago, seems
She mopped the floor up with these two. So let
Me just apologize again. Gert's

A whirlwind, 'specially when she thinks her baby
Sister's being picked on, but I hope
You won't hold that against her, judge, or me

Because, you know, she had a sort of rough
Upbringing, Irish family, lots of kids,
Six boys, then Gert, then me, I'm the baby,

All the boys loved to box, so Gert
Learned how, used to spar with 'em till soon
The younger ones refused to put the gloves on with her,

Said she hit too hard and wouldn't
Back off when the bell was rung. You see
The art of throwing leather was a part

Of family culture growing up, and even
After all these years—Lord, help me, judge!—
I still like a prizefight that isn't a fake.

Of course you do. What discerning person doesn't?
Indeed, and tell me, Mrs. Fish,
Why is it I'm inclined to think you also

Like the rowing on Central Park Lake, love the theater
But never come late (unlike a date
In court), never bother with people you'd hate?

Why is it that I think that, Mrs. Fish?
Now, Fox, that'll be enough of that,
Recall I said before, all comments here're

From the heart—not from Rodgers and Hart.
Oh, that's all right, your honor, I know men,
Know how inadequate Bill's Mr. Fox

Must feel getting roughed up by a girl
Like Sis, know he'd never dare try any
Funny stuff with her, so he takes

It out on me, cracking wise—cheap shots
Is all. Say, listen, I've seen his kind in spades.
But getting back to what you asked before—

How it came to this, what went wrong
With Bill and me, I don't know's I could say it
So's you'd understand, don't know, judge, if I

Understand myself. Maybe if I
Start at the beginning it'll all
Come clear. Well, first of all, Bill's older than me,

First time we met he was fifteen, I
Was ten. Billy he was then, played second
Base, sometimes maybe shortstop, on a

Ball team with my brother Pat, but Billy
He stood out. You know how teenage boys'll
Get to acting snotty with kid sisters,

Trying to make out they're grown up and you're
A twerp, it's "Get lost, squirt, go chase yourself,"
Or else "Go home, baby teeth, your momma's

Callin'." Well, sir, Bill was never like that,
Never mean, he'd take the time, talk
To me just like I was a person, not this

Drip, and when he'd see me on the street,
Maybe walking with my girlfriends home
From school and I'd say, "Hello, Billy," always

He'd say, "Hello, Mary Marg'ret, how's
The kid?" Well, when you're young and someone
        treats you
Like a person, that's a compliment

You don't forget, not ever, 'specially
A girl. So Bill was just around, mostly
With my brother, always nice, always

Kind of quiet, then fresh out of school,
He ups and joins the Marines—surprised
Most folks, him being so mild-mannered, almost shy,

Still, his dad had fought on Iwo Jima, so,
Seemed nothing else would do
Except, like him, he had to be a mud

Marine. That first time Bill dropped by in his
Dress blues—well, sir, you know that phrase
"Be still, my heart"? I'd turned fourteen the day before,

Some friends were over watching Bandstand on
TV when Bill showed up, looking for
My brother Pat who'd left, but Bill

Just sat down anyway, told us all
About his basic training, laughing, kidding,
Telling stories on himself, and god!

Was he handsome in that uniform,
Confident, grown-up. You think my girlfriends
Didn't notice, didn't think Miss Mary Marg'ret

Was the tuffest, teasing me some
Later, saying "Yes, I bet he came
To visit Pat"? Oh, I was something those days

(Though you might not think to look it now),
Full-figured, developed early. Well, sir, Bill
Was off in the Marines, time to time

He'd write Pat how he loved the life (thought maybe
He might make it a career), and always
With a postscript meant for me, some nonsense.

Later on, winter '67/
'68, his outfit got assigned
To Vietnam, and Pat stopped getting letters.

All of us were worried with no news,
That's why it almost came as a relief
Hearing he'd been hit by shrapnel near

Khe Sanh, not bad enough to send him home,
He finished up his tour there, but never
Mentioned staying in anymore once they'd

Shipped him stateside and he'd started
Writing Pat again. In fact when he
Got back to town, we didn't see Bill much,

He'd changed, folks said, kept mostly to himself,
No more joking, quieter than before.
I thought maybe I'd done something made him

Mad, that's 'cause the postscripts meant for me
Were missing when his letters started up
Again, and then one day, after he'd

Been home a while, I passed his parents' house
And Bill was sitting on the front steps, kind of
Looking off in space, so I said, "Hello,

Billy, how's the kid?", then kept on walking,
Seeing would he say hello, but seemed he
Didn't want to hear, so I went back,

Sat down right beside him on the steps,
Said, "Billy, tell the truth, did I do something
Ticked you off?", well, when he wouldn't answer

Even then, instead just looked down at the ground,
I felt invisible as air,
Pushy, dumb, that's when I saw these teardrops

Streaming down his cheeks, and him just sitting there,
Not moving. Well, I reached out, ran
My hand along his arm and said, "Billy,

It's all right, oh, Billy, it's all right."
I couldn't think what else to say, he just
Kept crying so, and all I could get out of him

Was how he'd let his buddies down.
I thought maybe he felt ashamed 'cause he'd
Come back and lots of those he'd gone with

Hadn't—leastways that's what I thought then,
But when those silent spells would capture him
At times, years later on, well, then I thought

The cause went deeper, thought, judge, what he'd found
Out there, wading waist-deep in some wet
Rotting jungle was that even if

You're young and tough, determined and American,
Still, no strong grip's strong enough to haul your
Best friend back up from the mud

Once his grip goes slack and he's deadweight.
But what's that say except Bill learned the limits
There of being human? Something each

Of us has got to learn in time, though seems
To me we shouldn't have to start that soon,
Away from home, dirty, sleepless, scared, no,

Shouldn't have to, judge, because each life
Deserves at first some room for plans, illusions,
Crazy expectations, a time we think

We're never going to die and nothing we
Can dream's beyond our reach, because, you know,
Without a time like that, what life won't seem

Too long, seem too much of a piece? At any rate,
We spent that afternoon just sitting
On the steps, me talking, Bill beside me

Maybe nodding now and then at something, once he'd
Got a grip on his emotions.
Well, after that, you know, it wasn't any time

Before we started going out,
Having coffee, taking walks, he'd talk
About how hard it was, getting back

To where he'd been before, how nothing seemed
Important, everything was kid stuff here
Compared to what he'd done in-country there,

And even if he couldn't see his ever
Living sixteen months like that again,
Still, there'd been enough stray moments of

Adrenalin, a common closeness, each
One counting on the other's knowing how to
Do his job, that shared elation when you'd

See the sunrise, surprised to find yourself
Among the living after hours spent just
Hanging on, not getting overrun,

Hours where you'd won the freedom of
The dead, crossing yourselves off as goners
Half-a-dozen times there in the dark,

Only to have that freedom fade as your
First meal revived you just enough to be
Afraid again of dying. Well, sir, Bill said

After what he'd gone through out in 'Nam,
He knew no matter what he did when he
Got back, he'd never feel alive as that again,

Never feel he'd live his life so
"All the way up" as he did there.
Well, judge, I ask you, there I was eighteen,

Starting college at St. Mary's here in town,
Thinking I might major in the classics
'Cause I'd always liked mythology

And Mom said go ahead, that college for
A girl was where you'd get to do things (maybe
For the last time in your life) just for

You alone, just because you liked them,
Told me not to waste time taking subjects
Meant to help me get a job, she'd give me

All the practical instruction I could
Use and said just one of her eight kids
Was going to end up cultured if it killed her

So it might as well be me, that learning
Latin like a priest was classy (prob'bly
Why they called it classics, huh?) and if

I turned up talking Greek around the house,
My pop would faint, and that's a thing she'd like
To see. Well there I was, with all that still

Before me, when Bill Fish here lets his hair down
On our walks and says he'll never feel alive again
As when he thought sure he was dead.

Well, golly, what's that mean? How's a girl
Respond to that—"Have another cup of
Coffee, Billy"? That's the sort of thing

Mom always tried with Pop when he'd start shouting
How a man's life's got no meaning, how
There isn't any justice in the universe,

And didn't she think so?, because Mom said
When Pop had asked her that the first
Few times, and she'd obliged by saying what

She thought, that he'd just look at her like she
Was nuts or else he'd wonder out loud to
Himself why women couldn't seem to grasp

The deeper things in life, that's when she said
She'd realized when men go on like that,
Then ask you what you think, don't answer, give them

Something good to eat, 'cause when they start
Complaining how the world mistreats 'em, doesn't
Understand 'em, well, it doesn't mean

Much more than when a baby starts to cry,
They don't want conversation, they want soothing, see,
Want something nice and warm stuck in

Their mouths, and sure enough, my pop would always
Calm down quick from ranting when she'd slide
A slice of cobbler in his gob. Well, that's

My mother, judge, but that's not me. I figure
Billy tells me what he's feeling, he
Expects I'll do the same, doesn't think

I'm just a wailing wall with hair. So I
Say, Billy, think about it this way, maybe
What went on out there in 'Nam wasn't

Any picnic, still, it couldn't be
Much worse than what your dad went through on Iwo
Jima, he came back, got a job,

Raised his kids. Lots of people get
Bad breaks, sure, but maybe if we each've got
Our share of trouble coming, it's

The lucky ones run up against it when
They're young, resilient still, strong enough to
Get themselves beyond it. All I know's

Whatever happened out there, terrifying,
Ugly, numbing, or exciting even,
It was only an exception, Billy.

No one leads their life according to
Exceptions. Sameness, some routine's the concrete
Days are made of, playing notes the way

They're written, finding true things where you'd
    left them.
Dull and daily does it, Billy, someone
Says in Dickens, 'cause deep down inside

The everyday's a vein of sweetness, plain
Contentment that, my mother used to say,
You've got to mine your way to, digging tooth

And nail—that's what I said to Billy, judge,
Every time we talked six months running till he
Finally got the point and figured

Maybe he could use the G.I. Bill,
Go to college, then the two of us'd
Be the first in both our families made the

Grade. Well, within a year he'd started
State, planned to major in accounting,
Though he changed in junior year to business.

We dated off and on through college, not
Exclusively of course since he was off
In College Park, I finished my degree

A year ahead of Bill, 'cause I'd started
One year sooner, as I said, then taught
In elementary school while Billy

Finished up his bachelor's, looked for work,
And got a job here in insurance. Soon
He started talking marriage. Well, you know,

Bill was always sweet and gentle, thoughtful,
Always made me laugh, but wasn't, judge,
To tell the truth, the great love of my life, no.

That one was a boy I met in college
With eyes bleak and cold as the North Sea, not
That I've ever seen the North Sea, you know,

But that's the way the hero in a book
I read once looked who touched my heart just like
Ignatius did. At any rate, I ended up

Hopelessly in love, although I
Never knew for sure, sir, if he understood
How much I cared, or cared himself.

And being shy, I'd never dared to speak
My feelings first, and then the summer after
Sophomore year he left for home and didn't

Come back in the fall. I never knew
For sure what happened, never saw the boy
Again. It nearly broke my heart, but Mom said . . .

Excuse me for a moment, Mrs. Fish,
But Mr. Fox keeps gesturing at me
With this big ferocious look. Yes, Fox?

Forgive the interruption, sir, but might I
Have a word aside with you and Bird?
It'll only take a moment, please.

All right, but make it quick. Why don't we three
Just step into the cloakroom here. Excuse us,
Fishes, if you will. . . . Well, Fox, what's up?

Good grief, judge! this gal is dull as dust
And slower than molasses in the winter with her
Billy this and Billy that

And dear old Mom the other. Now here comes
This great lost love who's vanished, prob'bly fell
Into the sausage grinder working summers

At the packing plant—that step, or some such
Equally disarming pas de faux.
Imagine, judge, the scene as in a Bab

Cartoon illuminating mordant verses
Titled "Sweet Ignatius in the Grinder's
Maw": a pen-and-ink line drawing shows

A cruel machine, fitted with a funnel,
Out of which protrude two legs whose wildly
Wagging feet wear Keds. Meanwhile, in the distance,

Leaning out a tower window
Letting down her golden hair, observe
A younger, stricken Mrs. Fish. Oh, by

The way, her lost love's eyes may well be "bleak
And cold," but since his head's not showing, how
Are we supposed to know? If that, sir, were

The tale she had to tell, at least the thing
Might be diverting, but here this gal's been jawing
On and on, explaining, judge, ab ovo

How her marriage fell apart, albeit her
Rendition hasn't even got
Them married yet. Can't we move this thing

Along, can't we keep her to the point?
After all, I've got three sets of kids
By diff'rent ex's, sir, I pay support for, so

I simply can't afford to spend this time
While she rewinds the story of her life,
And when it comes to that, what is there

To know—that women's lives are boring (filled
With recipes and carpools, new curtains for
The kitchen)? I didn't marry five of 'em,

God knows, not to grasp at least that fact.
Yet here's a gal glories in "the dull
And daily," well, she's got that first part nailed.

Mr. Fox, it's fortunate you sought
This sidebar out of earshot of the Fishes.
Had you made these comments with the others

Present, I'd've had to reprimand you,
Maybe hold you in contempt. Where
Do you get off, dismissing people's lives

Like that, implying ordinary, honest
Folk whose days lack vivid incident or
High emprise aren't worth a hoot, or did I

Read too much into your image "dull as
Dust" applied to Mrs. Fish? And weren't
You, Fox, the one here recently reciting

Odes to bailiffs, "little folk whose lives
Are often empty and banal," if I
Recall your words correctly, though those lives

Seemed grand enough, I'd wager, once they'd laid them
On the line to save your skin. If shame were what
It used to be, you'd be walking with

A limp for days. Now we're going back
Again and hear the rest of Mrs. Fish's
Side, and let me warn you, Fox, there'll be

No eyebrow raising, eyeball rolling, sighing,
Any such like, or, as God's my witness,
Fox, I'll throw a Buick at you, understand?

You tell him, judge. I told *him*, Mr.
Bird, and see to it when Mr. Fish
Begins his version next, I don't have cause

To tell you much the same. Let's go. . . . Well, Fishes,
Here we are again, forgive the interruption.
You were saying, Mrs. Fish, when your

Husband found a job and started talking marriage,
That's the time you realized this other
Young man, Aloysius . . . No. Ignatius . . .

Yes, of course, how stupid of me, this
Ignatius, in contrast to Bill Fish here, was,
In fact, the great love of your life, correct?

Yes, judge, but don't you know, that doesn't mean
I didn't love Bill Fish. I did. And when
It comes down to a life's great love, well now,

How many of us get to marry that one?
It's that "might have been" people keep
To make them think their lives presented

Possibilities they never really did.
I learned that years ago, and only brought up
Here the way I'd felt about Ignatius

So's you'd know my state of mind, judge, when
I said I'd marry Bill, know I'd taken
Mom's advice about how life's just one long

Compromise and most folks make their big one
Choosing whom to marry, that a girl
Can waste a lifetime waiting for Mr. Right,

And how it's women are the ones, she'd say,
Make a marriage last, since marriages are
Marathons and men mainly sprinters.

Well, you can see, judge, how a girl'd get
To thinking happiness depended on
Adjusting expectations, 'cause there's no one

Ever gets in life everything
They want, while others never seem to get
A single thing they aim for, no, but in

Between the two where most folks live, it's all
A trade-off, that's to say, in marriage (though
I didn't think about it that way till some

Years had passed) how much can you expect
Another to give up, out of their own and only
Lifetime, getting you the life

You'd like, giving you the sort of thing
You'd always hoped for? Then, how much of yours
Must you give up in turn, making theirs

Come out the way they want? You see, that seemed
To me in time the deeper sense, sir, of
"Adjusting expectations." At any rate

My mom said, "Look, we've known Bill Fish's family
Since the two of you were pups and always
Liked 'em fine, and that's not nothin' 'cause when

"People marry, Meg, their families marry
Too. Besides we know Bill's brave and gentle,
Comes by things like that from both his folks,

"And haven't you been friends since grade school, best
Friends for a while now? Listen, that's a better
Base to build a marriage on than rare,

"Romantic notions young girls get from reading
Books, daydreaming afternoons in their bedrooms
After school. And don't you for a

"Moment underrate the fact he makes you
Laugh, that's saved more marriages than all
The fancy-pants psychology folks talk,

"And later, Mary Marg'ret, when the babies
Start to come, if Bill turns out to be just
Half the dad his own pop was, well, you'll learn

"To love him more than any boy that's named
Ignatius who, I'd bet, was just some little
Sharp, hair-splitting Jesuit down deep."

Well, judge, I married Bill—I guess you've gathered
That by now—and for the first few years
We couldn't have been happier, sky high

The way young people are just starting out,
Making plans, making love. Our first
Apartment wasn't big enough to swing

A cat, so always we were in each other's
Way, but what's that matter when the person
In your way's the one you want to see

The most, matter when the world and both
Of you are free and fresh still to the touch of
Summer skins, the velvet tease and taste

Of two rough tongues, till every evening after
Work's a race (comic, randy, maybe
Crazed, depending where you're standing) just

To get back to the other and to bed.
How long's it last like that? Six months,
Perhaps a year, but after that it's got to taper

Off, else you'd both collapse from lack
Of sleep, that or find (worse luck), as Bill
Said years ago, there's only so many ways

To put a peg in a hole. But what's that mean
Except that when the tidal wave of romance
Washes over you and past, you've got to

Build again each day's routine, resume
The life you'd lately led, only this time
With a person bound by oath to split

The load, take up the slack and such, and so
That's when we started out, I guess, on our long
Journey here, hope slung across our backs.

Bill set to work, got his first promotion
While I taught another year, then quit
To go to nursing school. God, but we

Were strapped. I still remember how we'd saved
To get a sofa, then an easy chair
Small enough to fit that space we airily

Referred to as "the living room" between
The hall and breakfast nook, remember how,
When this other couple came to dinner there

The first time and we'd put them in
The place of honor on the couch, Bill in
His easy chair, me perched on its arm,

I said I needed to be up and down
Checking on the dinner so I didn't
Want a chair, as if we could've wedged

Another in that alcove. Who was I fooling?
But that's the way I thought a wife behaved,
Made excuses, sacrifices, just so

Things turned out all right, and that was fine
With me, but when the husband of the other
Couple had too much to drink and spilled

A glass of red wine on the sofa, well,
I could've cried from pure frustration then
And there, but ran instead to get the talcum

Powder for the spot, saying it was
Just an old sofa anyway
And didn't matter. It's funny, judge,

About possessions, objects stained for decades with
Dumb feelings. Take that sofa, for example,
First big thing we'd bought together, first thing

That was "ours," it made us feel, even
After we'd been married almost for
A year, really grown-up. Funny how

Some furniture'll follow you from place
To place through life yet seem to wander, as
You go along, from room to room. That sofa,

Judge, that started out stuck in our tiny
Living room'd made it, by the time
We took the new apartment three years later,

To the space we called Bill's study, then
It went upstairs to Stephen's bedroom when
We bought the house and stayed there almost sixteen

Years. It's in the attic now, but when
The Goodwill came I couldn't throw it out,
Meaning as it did to me younger,

Happier days. You know, judge, we were never
Quite as close again as those first years
Struggling to get by, as close as when

That two-seat sofa represented something
Really valuable in terms of what
It took to earn it, hope become reality.

I think (and, judge, I've done a lot of thinking
Lately seems) how folks so often'll
Accumulate possessions as a way of

Keeping score, seeing are they better off
Than mom and dad at that same age, whether
They're ahead, or leastways, even with,

Their neighbors, folks they work with, only later
Looking back, realizing most of
What they'd gotten simply served to give

Time's liquid moments weight, some space where life's
Bright foam could pool and linger in a thing,
Not run away like moonlight through your fingers,

Objects able to soak up the past,
So when you got to thinking back about
Your life, uncertain what was mem'ry, what

Was dream, you'd only have to look around you,
See some leather chair, a lamp, a figure on
A mantle maybe, then recall

Its where and when and know at least some moments
Weren't unreal, yet understand as well
How time speeds up the farther on you get,

How, with wealth, possessions multiply,
Can seem indiff'rent, interchangeable,
Grow lighter, getting ready for that instant

When the objects you've collected through
A lifetime, just like that! no longer know you,
Wheel and float away like wood chips on

A stream. Well, judge, I don't know I can say
Just what I mean, or if I could, whether
You'd understand. At any rate, I've prob'bly

Lost the thread, telling how things happened.
Let me see, I finished nursing school
(Three years here in town at old St. Joe's),

Got my R.N., passed the state exam,
Then took up pediatric nursing. Meanwhile
Bill was thriving, going great guns at

The office, seems he had this natural talent,
Motivating, managing, that sort
Of thing—Bill said his training in the Corps's

What made the diff'rence. His boss'd give him all
The special jobs to handle: tricky cases,
Troubleshooting, not a one he didn't

Tackle, didn't straighten out. Of course,
The more success he had, the more he liked
His work, liked it maybe too much, seemed

JOHN
BRICUTH

98

To me, judging by the hours he was
Spending at the office. That's because
The way most guys got ahead, Bill said,

Was being at their desks before the boss
Showed up for work so he could see 'em when
He came, then staying late (a minute past

The time the boss went home), so he could see 'em
When he left. A stupid trick, but Bill said
Stupid tricks'll often work and if

The others played it that way, well, you know,
He couldn't afford, sir, not to play it too,
Besides his dad had told him how in business

If you ever had to choose between just
Being right and looking right, always
Choose to look right, see, 'cause otherwise

You'd never get a job where being right could
Make a diff'rence. Well, Bill had said he wasn't
Quite as cynical as that yet, still

These people were the ones he had to work with
So he couldn't look too different starting out.
Let's see, by that point we'd been married

Just about five years, we'd settled in
The new apartment, started planning for
A family, then within that summer I got

Pregnant. Well, judge, you should have seen Bill here:
First month he bought a crib, a playpen, then
He thought he'd paint and paper our spare bedroom

For a nursery, picked the paper out
Himself: baby elephants, balanced on
Their hind legs on a ball, holding

Pink and blue banners in their trunks.
Of course, when Bill tried to get it on the
Walls, he made a mess. We had to call

A paper hanger, fixed it up professionally
That quick! and then, three months in,
I lost the baby. Well, you've got to understand,

That's the first really bad thing
Ever happened in my life. There I was,
Almost twenty-eight, both parents

Still alive, brothers, sister too
(Never knew my four grandparents—they'd
All died before my birth), so till that point

I'd never lost a person I was close to,
Didn't think, like most young people, death
Could ever touch me, let alone, reach

Inside to harm a dreaming thing
That couldn't even whimper—I was wrong.
Even Bill who'd seen so much of death

So young was stunned, kept saying how by fixing
Up the nursery in advance maybe
He'd been guilty of presumption (never

Taking liberties, you see, not showing
Off—always very big with Bill's
Whole family), still, what I could never figure

Out was how, by simply making
Preparations so's to show a little timid,
Wide-eyed creature, "Look, it's not so frightening

Here," how we'd presumed, your honor, or
On whom. Mom said, "Mary Marg'ret, these things
Happen." Swell—but *this* thing happened to me.

And maybe she was right saying time
Would make it hurt less—yes, but how is that
A comfort, knowing no emotion, human

Feeling good or bad, resists that pitiless
Erosion? Anyway, time passed
(Whatever else it did), another year

Or so and I was pregnant once again.
Both of us were happy, sure, though Bill
Tried not to show it, said we shouldn't get

Our hopes too high, didn't want to jinx it, so
We tried to keep the same routine,
I rested more, watched my diet, made

An effort not to get too stressed or tired, and then,
Along about the fourth month I
Miscarried. Well, sir, I was beaten. That one

Almost did me in—not physically,
You know, but the other thing. I got
So blue, felt so empty, worthless—what

Women had been doing since time's start,
What any woman in a backward country
Does, lying in a ditch beside

The road, I couldn't seem to do. My mom
Was always fond of saying, "Children're
Life's meaning." Maybe so. Maybe if

That's right, my life would have to do without's
What I thought, and why, judge, once the shock
Wore off, I threw myself down a well

Of sorrow so deep I thought sure no one
Could follow, let alone try to find me,
But Bill found me, held me in his arms

In bed each night, rocked me while I sobbed
The way a child of two or three does till it
Gasps to catch its breath, then whispered how

He loved me, how it made no diff'rence if
We never had a child, that maybe we'd
Adopt, but all that finally mattered was

Us two, said things like that night after night
The way you'd do to sooth a restless or
Unruly kid to sleep, and then by day

He'd find occasions for a dozen thoughtful
Things, like when we'd first begun to date—
Phone calls, flowers, a quick admiring glance—

So I wouldn't feel like such a failure.
Simple as it was it got me past
The worst and, judge, whatever happened later,

I'll always say he saved my life in those
Bad days, showed me how a marriage makes
A history, gets its staying power: Sex is

Good, but tenderness and trust take root in nights
Like those, heartbroken in his arms—that,
And knowing in the world there's one who's

For you, one who's on your side as much
Or more than you are for yourself. That's
What makes the diff'rence, judge. Eighteen months

And I was pregnant once again, feeling
Sure if something happened to the baby
This time I was done for. Bill and I had

Talked it over, figured if I quit
My job, just stayed home, tried to rest
In bed, much as I could take, maybe

Mom and Gert could alternate on weekdays,
Helping with the meals, cleaning up
The house, Bill could handle weekends well

Enough, and though we'd miss my salary just
At first, still somehow we'd get by. Then Bill
Tried something else: one weekend he redid

The nursery, painted over all the papered walls,
Gave the playpen and the crib away to
Friends who'd just had their first child (same couple,

Judge, whose husband spilled the red wine on
The sofa), did that 'cause we both decided
With this baby we'd start fresh, keeping

Nothing from the past, not taking things
For granted. Well, the only hitch
Was Bill here couldn't stand Gert's cooking, nights

When she'd fix supper he'd just pick at everything
Laid on his plate, sniff it, then
Make faces till Sis nearly popped. Well, this

One night Gert serves up, sir, every single
Dish Bill Fish hates most: boiled tongue,
Stewed okra, rhubarb pie with buttermilk,

Puts them on the table front of Bill,
Then asks him if there's something she'd forgot
He'd like for dinner. Bill just smiles, doesn't

Say a word, looks at all the dishes
One by one pretending like he can't
Make up his mind and then as if what's missing'd

Suddenly just dawned on him, he says,
"Why, yes, Gert—a bucket." Well, you'd think
He'd slapped her right across the face. Gert

Lets out this moan, turns into a howl,
Then starts around the table after Bill,
So he jumps up, grabs the ketchup bottle

By the neck, set to clip her head
First sign of any rough stuff, though, sir, Bill said
Later how he'd only got the bottle

'Cause he thought sure Sis'd use it—I'm sure that
If I hadn't been there, more, been in
That delicate condition, there's no way that we'd've

Gotten Gert calmed down, and dinner
Might've ended badly, but, as things turned out,
Other than that one misstep our plan

Worked like a charm. Steve was born that spring—
Six weeks premature but healthy still.
And lord, judge, what a baby! Bill was buoyant,

Almost had to hold him down with ropes
Like one of those balloons, bouncing down
The street Thanksgiving Day. And me, well, I

Was justified, we'd passed the gift of life
Along. Before I'd failed, but not this time, no,
Now I had a son, someone special enough

I could spend a lifetime giving
Him the best I knew—firmness, understanding,
Unconditional love that makes

A boy so self-possessed, your honor, half
The battle of the day's already won
Each morning when he takes the bus for school.

Bill got concerned, thought maybe all the loving
I'd stored up, judge, from the first two that we'd
Lost would get poured over Stevie's head

Like some Niagara, thought maybe he'd be swamped.
But me, I wasn't scared, my mother told me,
"Just remember two true things—no one

Ever loved a child too much, and no one
Ever lied 'bout being lonely." Well,
Those first few years after Steve was born

Seem now the happiest in my life. One Sunday
In particular stands out, not
That something special happened, more because

It seemed so typical of days ahead,
Contentment I could count on, no
Extraordinary joy that flares up, then goes out,

No moment of intense elation like
Some mystics say they go through, no, just
An everyday expanding of the heart.

Stevie must've been no more than three
That Sunday Bill and I, holding
Both his hands between us, lifting him

At curbs, strolled down to the park and spent
The afternoon outdoors there, sitting on
The grass. We'd settled on the house the week

Before, and this day, well, judge, it was sweeping,
One of those in early fall, cloudless,
Crisp, with such a sheen on every leaf,

On every blade of grass, you'd think the world
Was minted fresh that morning. I'd a husband
That I loved who loved me more than he

Could say (or would), a shining child I'd won
My way to after being turned back twice,
And in a month we'd be in our new house,

So all that afternoon we played with Stevie—
Tag or hide-and-seek—until a little
Boy's hard-running weariness had tripped him up

And laid him sleeping in my lap.
Then Bill stretched out beside me yawning, dozing
Off. That's when, leaning back against

A tree trunk, watching leaves above me, worried
By a breeze, lift in waves and then
Subside, I listened close to what they'd whisper,

What they'd sigh, what birds would sing, mingled
With the distant hum of traffic from
The avenue along the park's far edge—

Sounds that seemed all meant to make me drowse,
And yet I kept awake, standing guard there
Over my small world thinking, Oh,

If only it could stay like this. And judge,
You know, for ten more years it did. I didn't
Start back working once again till Stevie'd

Entered first grade, not until I'd got
A schedule let me pick him up at school—
(I always figured moms should be there

For their kids when school let out). I wonder, judge,
If I've quite made you see the kind of child
Steve was, the young man he grew into—quiet

Mostly, rather listen anytime
Than talk, that's 'cause he loved to learn, and Lord!
How he could listen, sensitive you'd say,

A boy easily hurt by any sort of
Meanness, maybe that's what made him thoughtful
Well beyond his years, almost like

An adult when it came to sensing people's
Feelings, finding ways of showing that he
Cared what others felt. I can see

The look on Mr. Fox's face, dead certain
There's no mother of a son, let
Alone an only child, doesn't think

Her boy's the best. Maybe so, but Bill
Knows what I say is true. Steve was always
Special. Like this one time, sir, when he was

Five or six, I took him downtown with me
Shopping, big department store, crowded,
Steve got curious, first thing I know

He's wandered off, well, now, I figured, like
Most kids his age, once he looked around,
Didn't see his mother there, he'd panic,

Start to howl, and then I'd find him by
The uproar. So I wait, and nothing, not
A peep. That's when I got scared (so many

Nuts around), started walking up
And down the aisles looking could I see him
Anywhere, 'long about ten minutes later

Here he comes, calm as you please,
Looking this way, looking that. Well, when
I get through shaking him, he says, "Mommy,

What's the matter? You got lost. I hunted
For you. Weren't you scared?" Well, what could you do
    with a
Kid like that but love him? Maybe think

He's one who'll never quite need other people
Much as they need him—not aloof, sir,
Like my brothers said, stuck-up—just 'cause

He wasn't raised the same old roughhouse way
That they were, no, not Steve, he had this tender,
Loving heart that anything could touch, why

Once at Easter, not long after this,
Bill and I gave Steve a baby chick,
One of those spray-painted kind that's just

A blue-green ball of fuzz with matchstick legs,
But how that little boy adored it, called it
"Chuck," fed it, petted, played with it,

But you know, judge, once they're dyed, they never
Do survive, on purpose maybe, figuring
Parents wouldn't buy 'em if they knew

They had to raise 'em up. Anyway,
We had the chick three weeks, when this one
          morning
Steve comes in the kitchen set to feed it,

Looks inside the cardboard box, the chick's
Not moving. Steve says, "Chuck, get up, you Chuck"
(Because at first, you know, he doesn't get

What's wrong), picks it up, brings it where
I'm sitting, puts it in my hand gently
As he can, says, "Mommy, Chuck won't play."

I don't know what I said, prob'bly more
The way I looked made him know, sir, something
Bad had happened, puts his head down in

My lap and starts to cry, while I sit there,
The chick in one hand, Stevie's head beneath
The other, hearing him, voice muffled by

My skirt, sob half in question, half a plea,
"I didn't do it, Mommy, did I?", thinking,
As he said that, of the two I'd lost,

Those babies trapped in limbo who'd've been
His playmates, knowing if I couldn't understand
That yet or reconcile myself,

Then nothing I could say to Stevie now
Would seem the truth, so all I said was "Don't
Cry, Stevie, please don't cry." At any rate,

That evening after Bill got back from work
We put Chuck in a coffee can and buried him
In back, Bill dug the hole, Steve and I

Picked flowers, had a little funeral service there
That seemed to comfort Steve, although
For several days after, judge, he'd find me

At odd moments, stand there looking sad,
Want to know if anything he'd done had
Made Chuck die. That's just the kind of kid

He was, and sure, I guess you'd say if things
Like that're what stick in my mind from Steve's
First years, we must've had an awfully sunny life.

V

There's a saying: happy families
All are happy, judge, but in the same
Dull way. Well, maybe happiness is boring—

I can see by Mr. Fox's face
I'll get no argument on that one, still,
Compared, sir, to its opposite. . . . Perhaps

You've heard that Chinese curse current lately,
"May you live in int'resting times"? Well, 'long
About the year Steve turned thirteen, my times

Got int'resting enough. Bill was on
The fast track at the office, junior vice-
President, head of a division,

But that same year this bigger comp'ny tried
To take them over. Bill and several others
At his level, plus a lot of those

Below them, thought they'd prob'bly lose their jobs—
This larger firm was known for buying comp'nies up,
Then cutting their employees back

To boost the bottom line. Of course, I didn't
Know this at the time, Bill never brought
His business problems back home from the office,

Lot like his dad in that. "You don't upset
Your family over things they can't affect,"
He'd say. Why, Bill's mom didn't even know

His pop was laid off by the railroad till that
Morning he slept late and didn't go to
Work, took him six whole months to find

Another job, and then the railroad called him
Back, but since Bill's pop had always saved
His money . . . Well, as things turned out, Bill here

And several others from his office started
Meeting after work to have a drink,
Talk about their prospects, what they'd do if

They got fired. 'Course most of them had mortgages,
Kids in school, sometimes if they'd work late
They'd all go out to dinner, try

To figure their next move: hang on in hopes
The deal would flop, or if it didn't, take
A pay cut, put up with demotion just

To keep a job, that or right away
Start sending out their résumés, place
Their names with those recruiting firms, "headhunters"

I think they're called. Well, anyway, among this
Little group that met for dinner was
A woman, several years Bill's junior, level

Just below his own but in a diff'rent
Section of the comp'ny—no, I won't
Repeat her name, I wouldn't give her even

That much standing in my life. You see,
I only learned this later on, that Bill
And this young person at these after-hours

Gatherings always seemed to be the two
Who stayed the latest, had the most to say.
Bill told me afterwards, when I'd found out

What happened, how he'd been so worried over
Work, had longed to tell me all about it,
Talk it out, but felt he had to keep

It to himself, be strong for me and Steve,
Not seem a failure in his family's eyes,
That when he met this woman in the same boat

He was in, someone sympathetic,
A girl who knew the situation, felt
The same concerns, but not dependent on him,

No one he need feel a sense of
Obligation for, it made him feel less lonesome's
What he said, and why they seemed to hit

It off at once. Maybe so, but how
It went from those expressions of concern
To something more Bill wasn't sure, perhaps

Some desp'rate urge that people feel caught up
In situations looking lost, an urge
To throw off all restraints that rein in bad

Behavior, snatch at pleasure fast before
The axe can fall. Who knows? It could be that,
But prob'bly also due I'd bet—since I

Know men and know how much their sense of self
Gets bound up with their work (especially him)—
To Bill here feeling how he'd suddenly

Become a has-been in his forties after
Starting out so strong, and how, judge, if he lost
His job, he'd have to start again,

Start over, wond'ring if he'd maybe lost
A step, still had what it took, and I know
How a younger woman, once a man's

Become uncertain, represents the quickest
Way to prove he's still the man he was.
At any rate Bill said it lasted as a

Sexual affair not quite six months.
By then he felt so weighted down with guilt,
He had to break it off. But that's when *my* life

Turned ironic all at once, bent on
Having fun at my expense. Within
The year the firm that bought Bill's comp'ny

Started letting people go, but seems the man
Who made decisions where to cut had been
A mud Marine in 'Nam like Bill (must've

Seen that in his file in personnel),
And so not only was he not let go,
But six months later he was heading up

The same division, judge, within
The larger comp'ny. Bill's young woman'd been
Eliminated in the first quick round

Of firings—though I didn't know that yet,
Didn't know Bill had "a woman." Then
One weekend afternoon, your honor, I

Was in the kitchen fixing dinner—Bill
And Steve were in the backyard playing pitch-
And-catch (I could see them out the window

Just above the sink)—the telephone rang
And here's this person on the line I'd never
Heard of asking was I Mrs. William

Fish, said she'd been a colleague of
My husband at the office, wondered was it
True the things she'd heard: he'd been kept on,

Promoted even. I said yes. That's when
She told me there were details I should know.
Well, your honor, nothing but pure meanness

And revenge made her tell me all
The things she did. Seems she felt Bill should've
Done lots more to help her save her job

(When he was doing all he could to keep
His own), and when she'd heard he'd been promoted,
Well, she thought she'd call, have a chat,

"Just to spread the pain around" was what
She said. I don't know how the conversation
Ended, first thing I remember I was

Standing there, gripping the kitchen sink's
Cold edge, just trying to get the strength back in
My legs, staring through the window at

My husband, teen-aged son playing ball there
In the yard, thinking how not thirty
Minutes past my life'd been so full

Of good things, framed within that window, filled
With hope—that now seemed suddenly a lie.
You've had those dreams: you meet someone who's
    clearly

You, yet you're outside them watching, knowing
What they think's the real thing only looks
That way because they've always seen it through

A single pane. I wonder if a man
Can grasp how empty, insubstantial,
Intimate betrayal makes a woman feel—

This man who'd been my husband twenty years,
The father of my son, who'd touched me places,
Ways, no one ever had before,

Who'd been, besides, my closest friend
Since I was seventeen. Imagine for a
Moment how a breach of trust like that

Can tear you up inside, it's like
An earthquake drove a jagged spike of glass
Down deep into your chest, where any movement,

Even breathing, makes the angry edges
Grind against a bone or work their way
Inside some tender organ till there's no

Relief or letup, even for a minute, no—
Unless you find, in red successive
Waves of rage, welling up within you,

Melting shame, turning it to anger that
Like lava, seeping, clings to everything
And burns it black, some respite. I

Remember glancing down, sir, at my hands
(Noticing how white the knuckles were,
Distended almost) as if they might be someone

Else's. I remember trying to calm myself,
Think things out. Who was this woman anyway,
And why should I believe a word she said

When clearly what she wanted, judge, was simply
To make trouble, make Bill suffer? That's what
I thought, and yet she'd told me things about us

Only Bill could know, and then she'd ended,
"Don't believe me, ask your husband." That's
How sure she was, as if he'd never lie,

Not because he couldn't bear the thought
Of telling me a story, no, but more
Because she seemed to think their tawdry, hole-

And-corner love affair was something Bill
Had treasured up deep within his heart,
Too precious for him ever to deny it.

Honestly, I don't know how I made it
Through that afternoon, that evening, seems
To me I burned the blackened tuna steaks,

Then broke a glass setting up the table.
I know when Bill and Steve came in from playing,
Right away they sensed, sir, how upset

I was, especially Steve (he was always
Like that, like some animal that knows
When moods've changed simply by the flow

Of air across its skin), I could see it
In his eyes. I said I had a headache,
Bothered me so much I burnt the dinner,

Broke a glass, cut my finger—said that,
'Cause no matter how this hurtful thing
Affected Bill and me, not a word

Would get to Steve if I could help it, he'd
Still think his home was happy, same as always—
Not a breath to Steve, not anyone.

My God! if my six brothers ever learned
What Bill had done, Marine or no Marine,
They'd've killed him, not to mention what

My sister would've tried. I don't know whether you're
Much used to small talk with your dinner—
Me, I've always liked it, liked to sit and chat

About the day. Thank God that evening
Steve and Bill did all the talking. Now and
Then I'd nod, say a word, but if

You'd asked me what the conversation was
About, I couldn't've said. After dinner
When the dishes had been cleared and Stevie'd

Gone to watch TV, I said I'd like
To sit out in the backyard, smoke a cigarette—
Would Bill come too? It was one of those warm

Nights in summer, stars like silver talcum
Blown across the sky, weary, watchful,
We sat in lawn chairs, sat in silence there

The longest time, then I began to talk.
He didn't deny a thing, your honor, told me
How ashamed he was, sorry almost

From the start, how the strain of maybe
Getting fired (he's always had this deep,
Exaggerated fear of failure) made him

Go a little crazy, made him try
To validate his worth, sir, with a stranger,
But, he said, the whole affair was simply

Sexual—in his heart it didn't mean
A thing. I couldn't stand it anymore,
I said it seemed to me the moment he'd

Begun this sleazy game our marriage was what
"In his heart didn't mean a thing."
How'd he ever let some worry over work

Eat away his self-respect enough he'd
Put our home, Steve's happiness and mine,
At risk? But then it seemed to me, sir, ever

Since the time when Bill's career began to soar,
Work was what he cared for most.
I told him that. And, judge, you know, he didn't

Fight that either, said that growing up
He'd got the sense, list'ning to his pop,
A wife and kids were things a guy might *have*

Or he might not, but for a man his work is
What he *is*. And Bill recalled whenever
Someone asked his mom what she was,

She'd say, "A wife and mother," but he'd never
Known his pop to answer that one any
Other way than "I'm a railroad man."

Maybe he was wrong, but that's the sense
He'd got. Well, there it was. I asked him did he
Realize we'd never get trust back like it'd

Been, that life for us would be this
Mended plate that couldn't take extremes
Of heat or cold, take any careless handling—

That's when I simply lost it, judge, I started
Sobbing, "Why, Bill, why, just tell me what
I did? Wasn't I a good wife? Why did

I deserve this kind of treatment? Tell me!"
He leaned across, held my hand, swore
No matter what it took, however long,

He'd make it up. I turned his hand over,
Held my cigarette just close enough
To singe the hairs, then said I'd like to stub it

Out there so he'd feel how much I hurt.
He said, if it would help, go ahead.
I threw his hand back, whispered, "Not that easy."

My family's Irish, judge, forgiving and
Forgetting's something we don't do so well,
It isn't in our genes. I told Bill Stevie

Mustn't ever learn the way his dad
Had shamed his mother, no; that he and I
Would work things out as best we could, but Stephen

Mustn't ever suffer 'cause of Bill's
Betrayal. So, starting there, sir, Bill
And I began to patch a life together.

What a dead'ning, hopeless business! Going
Your way daily, trying to pretend there's
Nothing changed, while watching the affection

Drain away: not seeking out the other
Soon as you'd get home, not sharing trifles,
Scraps of news, nonsense, maybe just a

Batch of fresh baked cookies (little things
It's true, but what's the sense of closeness mostly
Made of?), then the gradual letting go

Of this and that, till one day comes, you look up
From your book and find you're happier
Doing things without the other, that he's

The grit in every gear, the irritant
In making conversation. Hard enough!
But those long nights lying there in bed.

My God, I've never felt so lonesome in
My life, sensing in the silence how we each
Were curling up inside. And who

Was there to talk to, when my best friend was
The one who'd let me down? Not my family—
That was out—not some girlfriend who,

No matter how she'd sympathize, how close
She'd been for years, you see, might still let something
Slip among our friends. I couldn't take

The chance—Stevie overhearing gossip
In the neighborhood. (You know the sort
Of thing—pretending to commiserate,

While all the time unconsciously enjoying your
Distress, well, maybe not "enjoying," judge,
Just feeling smug about their lives compared

To yours.) I'd lie in bed at night, where bad thoughts
Black as gangrene've nothing to distract them,
Getting angrier and sadder, wond'ring

Why, if Bill and Stevie were the most
Important things in life for me, why we
Weren't that for him, why his career, concerns

About its getting sidetracked, seemed
To've pushed more precious things aside. Lying there
With all those feelings festering

Inside, I'd tell myself I had to get them
Out into the light, get them in
The open air or else they'd poison our

Relationship for good, but me . . . , well, judge,
I've never been the one could speak my needs.
That's when I'd think how wrong this whole thing
    was—

That he should stray, and I should plead. I've got
My pride. . . . *Now, Mrs. Fish, hold that thought*
A moment if you will, I think your lawyer

Wants to interject a word on your
Behalf. Yes, Bird, what's up? Might I speak with
You and Mr. Fox outside please for a

Minute, judge? *All right. Excuse us, Fishes,*
This shouldn't take us long. . . . Well, what's the matter
Now? You seem upset at something. Not

Requesting equal time, I hope, just 'cause
I granted Fox that earlier word aside?
No, sir, not at all. Still, didn't you

Admonish Mr. Fox on that occasion
Over lawyerly deportment here,
Proscribing, if my mem'ry serves, eyebrow-

Raising, eyeball-rolling, penny-ante
Antics of that sort, especially when
My client has the floor? And yet while she's

Recounting how her Billy Boy'd boinked
This hotty at the office, causing, if you'll
Note, grievous mental pain and suff'ring,

Why, sir, that's the very point opposing
Counsel picks to lean his head way back
Behind his client's chair (where only I

Can see his face), catch my eye, then stick
His finger down his throat—a gesture
Calculated to enrage, throw me off

My game, tempting me to some intemp'rate
Move that well might sink my client's case.
But did I bite on Fox's bait? Not even

For an instant. I maintained a glacial
Calm, if I do say so myself,
Merely giving Fox a look of cutting

Condescension, sad that such a fellow
Bears the honored name "attorney" here.
Yet even though his adolescent gesture

Couldn't faze, confuse, or fade me, still,
Since you'd explicitly forbidden such
Behavior, well, I thought you ought to know.

Oh, did you, Bird? I really wonder why if,
As you say, his making faces didn't
Bother you a bit—but never mind.

Now, Fox, I want to know about this trick.
Have you been bullyragging Bird again
After I'd expressly warned against it?

I'm the injured party here, your honor,
Not the lady, not the lady's lawyer, me
Alone, an innocent act grotesquely misconstrued

By Bird, thinking if he put me
In the wrong he could get the upper hand.
Well, here's what happened: earlier today,

Eating on the run, I grabbed a sandwich
(Philly steak with cheese, hold the onions)
From that Greek who runs the doggy wagon

Up the street. Well, sir, you're a man of the world,
You know how these things go, I got a strand
Of beef (gristle really) stuck between

Two molars (lower right, farthest back),
Didn't have a toothpick so I tried to
Work it loose with just my tongue but couldn't

Budge it. I was due here for this hearing,
So I came ahead, but then just like
A pebble in your shoe, that speck of beefsteak

Wedged between my teeth had gotten so
Annoying, judge, I simply couldn't concentrate,
Get my head back in the game

Given this distraction, so at what I
Took to be a lull in Mrs. Fish's tale
I leaned behind my client's chair, and with

My fingernail, pried the piece of gristle
Loose—that's the harmless gesture Mr.
Bird observed. And yet, God knows, I'm sure

I understand how Bird might reckon any
Reasonable adult, hearing Mrs.
Fish's maudlin screed, 'd feel an overwhelming

Need to hurl—but that's his thinking,
Judge, that's not my doing, no indeed.
Now listen, you two, whether this unhappy

*Couple's headed for divorce is something
Still to be decided, but there's one thing, boys,
That's certain, I'm divorcing both of you*

From ever showing up again together
In my chambers representing diff'rent
Sides. Now get back in there, quick. . . . Well, Mrs.

Fish, I think you'd said before, you didn't
Want your son affected by the trouble
With your husband, wanted Steve to feel

His home was still as happy as it had been
Always. Tell me, how did that work out?
Not so well. You know, judge, I was foolish

Thinking Stevie wouldn't notice things'd
Changed. He felt it from the first, but never
Guessed the reason far as I could tell.

What happened was we both grew closer: he set
Himself to cheer me up was how he saw it,
Make me feel less lonesome, less preoccupied,

And gradually his attitude
Toward Bill began to alter—not unfriendly,
Judge, but somehow just more guarded, like he

Wasn't sure how Bill would take to his
Becoming my best friend. So there we were—
Locked inside a compromise: Bill had

His work. I had my son. And Stevie—what
A sweetheart!, judge. You know, he'd go with me
To concerts, art museums, things Bill never

Cared about or always seemed too busy for when
Weekends rolled around, but things
Steve really liked. Most Saturdays, if Bill had

Gone down to the office, Steve and I
Would eat lunch out (the art museum cafe
Became our special place whenever new

Exhibits opened). Well, sir, I remember
One time Stevie at this Saturday lunch of ours'd
Tried to bring up what'd happened

In his roundabout, quiet way—whether
Anything he'd done had been the cause,
Whether Bill resented Steve's and my

Doing things without him. So I told him,
"Look, Steve, people change. You simply haven't
Lived enough years yet to know what time

Can do." He said he couldn't ever feature
Feeling diff'rent 'bout his dad and me
No matter how much time went by and asked

If we'd care less for him as he got older.
I said of course not—but I wasn't letting
Stevie draw me into conversations

Where I might let something slip. I finally
Told him not to worry anything he'd
Done had caused the present chill, he looked down

At his lap as if he'd been rebuked—
(I just this moment thought about the way
His eyelids always lowered when he felt

Ashamed—long lashes over eyes the deepest
Green you ever saw). And so he never
Brought it up again, just went on being

Mom's best pal. But then, you know, I had
Good reason to recall that conversation
Over lunch (about how people change

With time) because not three years after that
Steve's mood began to shift so, judge, it seemed,
When we'd do things together, it was more me now

Trying to cheer him up. It started
Senior year in high school near as I
Could tell, but then I never knew for sure what

Brought it on. I'd noticed all that fall how,
Soon as he'd get home from school, he'd head
Straight for his room, shut the door, then play

The same CD, hours on end—Gershwin's
Concerto in F—beautiful it was,
But mournful let me tell you, melancholy,

All that frenzied striving, reaching out for
Something just beyond your grasp, the yearning,
Then the sinking down, until the will's

Compelled, but never resignation, no—
A young man's take on life who'd felt how much
Heart's splendor lay ahead, and just how brief

The time might be to hold it. So, I'd stand
Outside his door, judge, listening to the music
Soaring, knowing what a boy his age

Would feel, since I'd seen it in my teenage
Brothers as a kid—that tumult of
Emotions fueled by pimples, sudden shyness,

Girls, the self's emerging sense of separateness,
Its need for privacy—why one time,
Judge, my brother Pat'd locked the bathroom

Door so long my pop went nuts, stood out
In the hall rattling the knob, shouting
Didn't he know that other people lived there too.

Poor Pat, you should've seen him skulking
Down the hall with Pop still fuming. When he
Passed me, sir, he made a sort of crackling

Sound walking, 'cause he had this magazine
He'd hidden underneath his shirt.
You see, I understood a boy Steve's age'd

Need some space to be alone, and him
As pensive as he was. But then that winter
Senior year he caught the flu, it turned

Into bronchitis first, then almost to
Pneumonia, seems he'd gotten run down, way
Too tired, staying up late nights reading.

Steve'd always been a reader, judge,
But suddenly that previous spring Steve's pastime
Turned obsessive, turned to somber books,

Russian novels thick as your fist. I'd see
The light below his door at night and then,
Come morning, dark circles underneath his eyes,

So I'd tell him, "Steve, you know—too much
Of a good thing . . . ," and he'd say, "Come on, Mom,
I've almost turned eighteen." Well, I mentioned

It to Bill but he'd already noticed,
So, come dinner, Bill goes on about how he's been
Gaining weight, could use some exercise,

Asked Stevie would he help, why didn't
They play pitch-and-catch again when he got
Home from work—that Steve could use it too.

He brightened up, said "Sure thing, Dad," but when
He looked across at me I knew he'd realized
How often Bill worked late, that what his dad'd

Said was wishful thinking, not a promise.
Anyhow I thought with all the things
That mothers of a teenage boy could worry over—

Drugs, dropping out, getting
Some girl pregnant—here's a kid who's staying
Up too late at night just reading books?

Was I nuts, fretting over what
My pop would call "luxurious regrets"?
But then, of course, Steve got the flu that winter,

Missed a lot of school home sick in bed.
Well, I admit I didn't mind that much, judge.
Seemed like he'd become a kid again,

I got to baby him, bring his meals up to
His room, we spent more time together.
You know, that's when I first began to sense this

Underlying sadness in my son, he'd lie there
With a fever, burning up, hair damp
With sweat, one long dark lock plastered against

His forehead looking for all the world more like
A splash of wet brown paint, and with this stare
That seemed to look so far away and deep

Inside, restless and weary both, I couldn't
Help recalling, judge, this young man in a
German book I'd started reading senior

Year in college (just some novel I mislaid
And never finished). You see, I thought
Steve's blues were over all the school he'd missed,

Afraid he wouldn't finish with his class, but
Once we got him well, I helped him catch up with his
Schoolwork so he made it through

On time. And then that summer what with all
The bustle getting Stevie ready for
His freshman year (he was heading off

To College Park—Bill's old alma mater),
Why, his mood just seemed to dissipate.
Came the day we loaded up the car to

Drive him to the dorm that first time, you'd've
Thought that Stephen Andrew Fish was some
Explorer heading off to reach the Pole.

'Course, I tried to hide how sad I felt,
But seemed to me he might at least've shown then
Some regret himself, leaving home

And mom. Instead he played the brave lad
For his father, talking all along
About what courses he could take, whether

He'd try out for Scitamard (the drama
Club), what his roommates'd be like.
I thought about the drive back home with Bill,

How it would seem to take us twice as long
Without Steve there, how Bill would sense my mood,
Try manufacturing conversation, only

To have it end up soon enough being
About the office. (You know, he never used to
Talk about his work, but after that thing

Happened, well, he started telling us
Come dinner time the day's events in detail,
Thinking probably his openness would

Reassure me, judge, those hours working
Late, the business he was doing, wasn't
Really monkey business.) So he talked

The whole way back about his job. I'd nod,
Say a word now and then. They'd given him
The oversight in bringing off

The comp'ny's next big acquisition (quite
A feather in his cap in fact), and if
He did it right, he "just might be the new

Executive VP," a job that in
Bill's firm had always been a sort of CEO-
In-waiting. Well, of course, he was excited,

Telling me about his plans. I didn't
Fall asleep, but then we're always not
Awake, sir, when our eyes are open, are we?

So, we came back to a house
Suddenly much larger than the one we'd left
That morning. I tried to fill the hours,

Occupy myself, I got my part-time job back
Nursing down at old St. Joe's. We didn't
Need the money, Bill was doing well,

Better than well, but goodness! I was lonesome
For Steve's comp'ny. Evenings were the worst—
Long when Bill worked late, longer when

He didn't. I'd call Steve every four or five
Days, sir, just to see how he was doing,
Pretending that I thought he might be lonely—

Sure, that fooled him!, like he didn't know who
The lonesome one would be. Well, I started
Planning Steve's Thanksgiving break the middle

Of September. Then when he came home,
What do you suppose? My little boy'd
Grown a moustache, judge. No mother likes

A moustache, 'specially not the first one, so
I teased him every chance I got, hoping
He might shave it off—but no. He'd gotten

Thinner too, and when I brought it up,
He said he had to stay up late nights lots,
Working on his courses, maybe that's

What did it. Come Thanksgiving day my brothers
Tom and Pat with their whole families came
To dinner, sat around the table laughing,

Talking, asking Stevie how it felt
To be a college man "out on his own."
Well, Steve'd never cared much for his uncles,

Always found them just a little crude,
And I could tell he thought that phrase "a man
Out on his own," implying he'd been pampered

Way too much growing up, was meant
To be a put-down, that's when Steve got silent,
One-word answers to their questions, yes

Or no, a sentence at the most, till Tom said
How he thought the cat'd got Steve's tongue,
When Pat chimes in, "May be—but looks to me

The caterpillar's got his upper lip."
They always kidded rough, my brothers did.
That weekend Steve went back to school, but it was

Just a month before the Christmas break
When he came home again and, judge, the change!
Thinner, yes, but with this look back in

His eyes I hadn't seen since he'd been sick
The previous winter, silent, almost sullen.
Well, we made it through that Christmas day,

But then the evening of the next day Steve
Asked Bill could he talk with him alone.
They spent almost two hours in the study.

Next morning Stevie said he thought he'd head
Back early, ride the bus back down to College Park,
Catch up on some schoolwork. Bill said

Steve'd got to feeling maybe college
Didn't make much sense for him, that maybe
He might learn a trade like landscape gardening

(As a kid he'd always loved to help me
Planting flowers). That's when Bill explained
How he and I had been the first in both

Our families ever went to college, how
We'd always thought we'd raised our people up
A notch, beyond the need to earn a living

With your hands. And what's a landscape gardener
Anyway? Just a fancy name
You'd give a yardman. Bill told Steve at last

How much it meant to both of us, having
Him in college. Couldn't he try harder?
Give the books another chance? So Stevie

Went back early—that next morning, judge.
But then the twenty-eighth, it must've been
About, oh, three A.M., the phone rang in

The bedroom. Well, you know the way that ringing
Late at night, jerking you from sleep
Before the fog of dreams has lifted, leaves you

Groggy, all defenses down, knowing
In a flash either it's some drunk
Or prank, but if it's not, no, if it's really

Meant for you, it's something bad. Bill took it
(Ever since Vietnam, when there'd be noise
At night, he'd come awake like that!), snapped

The bedside lamp on, sat there hunched, elbows
On his knees, feet on the floor—that's when
He says, "How bad?" and my heart freezes. Then

Again, "How bad?" (because whoever's on
The line's been taught that news like this can only
Break in stages), so Bill barks out, using

His ex-Marine's hard voice, "Stop it! Tell me now.
How bad?" And then, like some huge, useless
Marionette, wires cut at once, he simply

Slides down off the bed until he's sitting
On the floor, making helpless noises
In his throat. I started screaming then.

That night, your honor, most of that next day
All seems to blur together. What I could get
From Bill, once he could talk, didn't make

Much sense: Sometime after one A.M.
Steve Fish was found lying in the parking
Lot beside his dorm. First they thought

A car had hit him, then they thought he must've
Fallen from the building. (It's a high-rise
Dorm—eight stories.) How? I asked myself.

And then, Who said this boy was Stevie? Couldn't
They have made a bad mistake? We'd have to
Go there right this minute, see the body,

Prove it wasn't him. Where was this
ER? This "head nurse" who'd called?
Bill said he couldn't trust himself behind

The wheel, that's when he phoned my brother Pat.
Pat took us down. That whole long drive I kept
Repeating to myself the diff'rent ways

Mistakes were made identifying people,
Each one more fantastic, maybe just
More desp'rate, than the rest. I don't know, judge,

How much experience you've had
Seeing people who've just died a violent death.
I'd so convinced myself the boy they'd found

Couldn't possibly be Steve that when
I saw him on the gurney there I fainted.
They had him underneath a sheet with nothing on

Except his boxer shorts. The alcohol
They'd used to swab him down, dissolve
The dried blood caked around his nose and ears,

Had left its faint, evaporating smell still
Clinging to the sheet—last thing I
Remember there before I screamed

And slumped across the gurney—just like the color of
Steve's skin was what I noticed first when I
Came to. Stevie'd always had the fairest

Coloring (got that from my side)—that's what
Made the diff'rent shades stand out so: violet
Bruises turning blue, this chalky grey tinge

Everywhere, and in the hollows, body creases,
Yellow shadows looking faintly
Greenish under cold fluorescent light.

Those colors made me feel how far away
He'd gone already, when all I wanted was to
Hold him like I'd done when he was little,

When he'd cuddle in my lap, embracing
Every part, but when I bent to hug him,
Judge, I did a foolish thing, I flinched

Instinctively, thinking how those bruises
Would've hurt him with the weight of my
Embrace, my little boy. . . . That's when I simply

Started crying till I couldn't stop.
Pat stayed there with me while Bill found the doctor
Who'd first worked on Steve, talked to both

The ambulance attendants, next the campus
Cop who'd come across Steve lying in the
Parking lot. Bill was trying desperately

To understand what happened, judge,
As if at that point it could make a diff'rence,
Bring him back. You know, there must be this much

Benefit in having witnessed, when Bill
Wasn't more than just a boy himself,
So many young men dying, 'cause, sir, after

That first paralyzing moment when they'd
Phoned and Bill just couldn't seem to pull
Himself together well enough to drive,

He'd gotten calmer, stronger with each passing
Hour, controlled his feelings more and more
Dealing with the doctor, nurses, campus

Cops, behaving with this sweet, straightforward
Dignity. Still, I could see what he was
Doing there, the scene he'd started acting out:

In case these people thought Steve Fish
Was just some drunk or doper, some wild college
Student, spoiled and irresponsible,

Bill was showing them through his behavior
Just how wrong they were, showing them
What sort of stock Steve came from, the stuff his boy

Was made of, acting out a father standing up to
Save his son's good name. Pointless, maybe. . . .
Still . . . endearing. Through the fog

Inside my head I'd managed to make out
One phrase of what the cop had said to Bill:
"He didn't leave a note." My God!, I thought,

Was this man crazy? He thinks my Stevie jumped.
I started shouting at him till Pat had to
Wrap his arms around me so I wouldn't

Hit him. That's when Bill'd asked the doctor
If he'd give me something just to quiet me
Down. Then when we finally got back home

That morning, Bill called our family doctor
Wanting something strong to make me sleep.
Those next few days Bill handled everything

Alone: the autopsy results, the funeral
Home, arrangements for the burial Mass.
I heard him talking to the parish priest

By phone, telling him, no matter what
He might've heard, Steve's death was accidental.
I guess Bill thought there might be some objection

To his burial in the Church but, judge,
That sort of thing hasn't been the rule
Since we were kids. And what'd he think they'd do,

Bury my little boy beneath a crossroads
With a stake struck through his heart? Still when
He told the priest it was an accident

(I know Bill's every intonation), I could
Hear it in his voice how he didn't
Quite believe it. You see, he hadn't told me then

The other things the cop'd said that night.
Then at the funeral Mass they had me
Filled so full of stuff to calm me, stop me

Breaking down, I felt like I'd been sealed
Inside a diving bell, looking out
Through tinted glass. I'd see the people—my whole

Family, Bill's as well, friends, neighbors,
Colleagues from his office—see them talking,
Then an instant later, muffled and

Delayed, their words would reach me. Well, I know, sir,
At the service how I must've to the others
Seemed inert. I'd put on my dark

Glasses, not to hide how red my eyes were, not
Because the slightest thing would start me
Crying, judge, not even 'cause whatever

I was taking made my eyes so sensitive
To light, but just because a grief as great
As that one can't be shared. I couldn't make

Eye contact there with anyone that still
Believed in comfort, people who inhabited
A world where time could take this hurt away.

So though I might've on the outside seemed
Composed, on the inside I was screaming,
Screaming loudest where the priest says how,

On that last day, "God will wipe away
The tear from every eye." Nothing but empty
Words that didn't change a thing! My Stevie

Still was dead. I thought about the nightmare
I'd been having since it happened: I'm in the
Parking lot beside Steve's dorm when all at once

I see him falling, almost in slow
Motion like people do in dreams, so I
Start running, set to catch him in my arms

Or throw myself beneath his body, break
The fall, only now it's like I'm running in
Slow motion too, panting hard,

Gasping even, feeling my lungs'll burst
Before I get there, but making up the distance
All the same, nearly have him in

My arms, when suddenly his falling body
Speeds up with a jerk, hits the asphalt hard,
Then lies there twisted while I stand,

Arms outstretched, whisp'ring, "God!, my little
Boy, my little boy." Well, the service
Finally ended at the church, then at

The graveside as they lowered Stevie's casket
In the ground, it hit me all at once:
I'd never see my son again, sir—not

In daylight, not in darkness, not in
This world or the next. And as I thought that—Lord!,
I felt like I'd go mad if I stayed there.

I think I looked around me, feeling,
Judge, if only I could run far off,
Run fast ev'ry direction all at once and just

Keep going till I dropped, then maybe somehow . . .
I don't know what. I think I even took
A step before Bill grabbed my arm, afraid I

Might be fainting dead away. That's when I
Looked back toward the grave, the casket dropped
From sight, and there was nothing. After that,

An Irish wake, sir, back at the house. Bill had it
Catered, handled everything, I couldn't
Face it. After half an hour there

I had to go upstairs. . . . And so then . . .
How do you take up your life again,
Fool yourself you've got a future, once a thing

Like this has happened? Bill took off a week,
Stayed at home, we tried to talk about it,
Judge, but suddenly I'd find these

Uncontrollable, big tears sliding
Down my cheeks, and Bill would just fall silent.
It's then he told me all the other things

The cop had said: how Stevie hadn't gone out
His window, no, but off the roof, along
The side that faced the parking lot, and how

The door that led up there was always locked,
But there'd been workmen up that afternoon
Who'd left the door propped open. That's when
     someone

Put a piece of tape along the door edge
So the spring latch wouldn't catch. They'd found
A roll of matching tape in Stevie's pocket,

So they thought he'd planned to take his life.
But I told Bill, he could've just gone up there
For the view, fresh air, then tripped, he'd never

Do a thing like that on purpose, never
Get that down without him giving me
Some sign, asking me for help. Bill just

Shook his head. At any rate, after
That week ended Bill went back to work.
I tried a week later going back

Myself—my old part-time nursing job.
But I was having such a hard time sleeping
Nights, what with dreams that broke my heart or

Else with having to take a pill to knock me
Out or get me going, I was like
A zombie when I showed up there, dropping

Things, forgetting them, walking places
In a mist and with that sand-papered
Feeling in your eyes you get, judge, when

You haven't slept. And then one morning six
Weeks after that, I simply couldn't get up,
Couldn't get out of bed, I lay there trying

Hard to think of what I had to live for,
Not to fool myself with fantasies but figure
Something real that I could build a hope on,

See my way to happiness again since
Steve was dead. But there was nothing. So
I stayed in bed till Bill got home from work.

Then he just sat beside me talking (I was
Curled up in a ball, head beneath the covers),
Trying to get me up to have some dinner,

Take a shower, something. Well, he couldn't
Budge me. I was still like that next morning,
So he called the family doctor. I won't

Bore you, judge, with all the back and forth of
That next year, the diff'rent doctors, diff'rent
Drugs, the lengthy hospital stays. It all

Came down to this (I saw the diagnosis
In among some papers on Bill's desk,
Papers he was sending off as background

For the health insurance): "Manic-depressive
Illness, probably hereditary.
Onset triggered by a life event

(Severe reaction, foll'wing only child's
Decease)." Well, I remember thinking if it was
Hereditary, something running

In the family, Gert had got the manic,
I'd got all the rest. The doctors tested me
With lots of diff'rent drugs, strong stuff

Meant to counteract some "chemical
Imbalance in the brain." It took a while
To find the one that worked, but even then

The bottom line was still, as one shrink said,
I had to come to terms with Stevie's death,
"Had to get my head around it," otherwise

The drugs were just this hopeless rearguard
Action fought against despair. Well, I
Won't deny it now there were moments

During that sad year I felt I'd like
To end my life—but couldn't do it, no.
What always stopped me was my knowing people'd

Say it proved that Stevie's death was not
An accident, that suicide ran in
The family. No, I couldn't shame my son

That way. But what'd it mean "to get my head
Around it"? That somehow I'd assent to my child's
Dying at eighteen, accept that at

My age I'd never have another,
Reconcile myself to no grandchildren coming,
Maybe playing doting aunt to all

My brothers' kids until I'm old—when they
Could tell their children, "Poor Aunt Meg, so sad.
You'd have to know her story." I'm sorry, judge,

But I won't stand for that. . . . You know,
        sometimes now,
When I first awaken in the morning,
There for just an instant, Stevie's death's

Not quite so present to my mind. And then
I look around and just like that! it all
Comes flooding back—and with that free-fall anguish

I first felt the night I heard it, saw him
Lying on that gurney. No, I love
My son too much to say his death was fate,

God's will, some random roll of dice, I don't
Know what it was, I only know no explanation
Makes a diff'rence now. Still, if

I had to live on after this, how was
I to do it? I thought about that lots—
Until my head just ached—then this one day,

Sitting in a lawn chair in the sanatorium
Garden, bathed in that peculiar bleakness
Of hot sunlight at high noon, it all

Came clear. You know, your honor, someone said once
Life is like a movie: Tragic mostly
In the close-ups, always comic in

A long shot. That's the way my life had come
To seem—I felt just like those people stranded
In the film who'd come to Casablanca

For the waters. 'Cause you see, sir, when
It came to marriage, I'd been misinformed.
I knew it was a contract, knew we gave

Our word to stand beside each other so
No matter what life had in store we'd never
Have to face it all alone. I thought,

As years went by, that if I held my end up,
More than held it up, why, then I'd made
A bargain, judge, with life. But no. I learned

Through hard experience life hadn't been
A party to the deal, knew nothing of it.
That day, sitting in the garden's

Sunlight, what I saw was there were other
Ways to make the great refusal than self-murder.
Maybe I couldn't take my life,

But I could leave my life behind. That's when
I asked for this divorce, and Bill eventually
Moved out. He thought my whole decision

Didn't make much sense, some notion I'd
Get over soon enough, said Stevie's death
Had hurt him just as much as me, but 'stead of

Giving up and turning inward, he'd
Responsibilities he had to meet—
To me, and lots of others (seems

The acquisition closed, so Bill had got
His big promotion). Well, I told him all that
Might be true, I felt ashamed, but still

It didn't make a diff'rence. (Besides there's no one
Possibly can hurt as much, sir, as
A boy's own mother when he dies.) I said

For me and Bill to stay together now
Seemed nothing more than this huge monument
To mutual failure. That's where we left it. Maybe

It's my fault. I only know the two men
I cared most about in life, my husband
And my son, when things were going rough

And both'd felt they'd lost their way, somehow
Never figured they could come to me
And share it. Maybe it's my fault. At any

Rate, what's the worst can happen now
(Is there something more still left
For me to lose?)—that I get old, alone and lonely?

Could be then I'd end up feeling some
Of what my son had felt there standing on
That rooftop, so at least we'd share that last

Communion. And being alone's not so bad.
Why, you can see me any evening if you're
Walking down the alley on my block,

I'll be at the kitchen table, drinking coffee,
Maybe smoking a cigarette, listening
For the kids next door, see me through

The back porch window's lighted frame, head back,
Dressing gown around me, staring off
At something you can't see. No, not so bad

At all. And then suppose I die some day—
If there's a hell, they must have some place there
For those who, while they lived, deliberately

Refused to be consoled by worthless dreams
Of compensation, and if that place is close
To where the young ones go who've recklessly

Rejected life's first gift, to where they're kept, well . . .
Maybe that's the last illusion. Still,
By any measure that you use, my life

Has failed in everything I cared for most.
But like Bill said once, anyone who's born here
Knows down deep, whether something seems

A failure or success, at last that matters
Less to folks like us, as long, sir, as it's big.
Yet even by that standard I don't count.

My failure's only ordinary, coming
On me daily—through some dream of love.
Is that the sort of thing you wanted said?

*Well, yes. . . . Thank you, Mrs. Fish, you've been
Exceptionally forthcoming, sharing recollections,
Personal feelings. I can't speak*

*For others here, but certainly for me
I found your commentary, first to last,
Quite moving. Thank you for your trust.*

Yes, Mr. Fox, what's the matter now?
A word alone with you and Mr. Bird, sir?
Won't take but a minute—in the cloakroom.

*All right. Fishes, please excuse us. . . . Well, Fox,
Get on with it, we still have Mr. Fish
To hear. And weren't you hurrying off somewhere?*

Really, I must object, your honor. Nothing
Mrs. Fish has said here leads us to believe for
Half a minute she'd intended

Ent'ring these proceedings open to
Your honor's wishes, holding out the chance
Of reconciliation. No, instead

Her statement seems designed to prejudice
The court on her behalf when this whole matter
Comes to trial, elicit sympathy and such

Over her bad luck with men,
First that mythic "great lost love" who vanished
Up the chimney, then Bill Fish, tear-stained

And shell-shocked, whom she married on the
        rebound
From the Cong, and last that son—I'd say
She'd ruined that one almost surely. (You know,

I met him once: not Marine Corps mettle
Like his father—rather, how to phrase it?, more
The corps de ballet.) And notice too

How artfully her narrative's constructed,
Hewing to the rule of three so prevalent
In fairy tales: First the car

Is dead. Then the phone is dead. Now
The son is dead? What's next, Mr. Bird?
The extraordinary rule of four? Was Mrs. Fish

Struck by a city bus while walking down
The hall outside? I'm sure we'd like to know.
Mr. Fox, have you no shame? Until

*This moment here I'd never really understood
The full depth of your cruelty. May God
Forgive you, Fox, your soul's at risk. Now get*

*Your butt back in there. God knows what the Fishes
Must be thinking! . . . Here we are again.
It's your turn, Mr. Fish. Go right ahead.*

VI

Well, your honor, most of what my wife just
Said is so. We met as kids, and by
The time she'd turned thirteen, I'd been a goner

For a year or more. You know, judge, I'd
Forgotten all about that stopping by
Her house fresh out of boot camp, wearing

My dress blues, making like I'd come to see
Her brother (though I knew she'd know I hadn't),
Did that so I'd leave a picture strong

Enough to last till I got back, then touched
It up with letters sent to Pat that always
Managed mentioning her name. Then I

Got sent to 'Nam, caught some shrapnel like
She said. This one night, judge, the dinks came
    sifting
Through the wire, hit our slit trench with an

RPG, and really lit us up.
I was half asleep, half awake
(A guy named Bradshaw had the watch), this thump!

And when I looked around, the upper half
Of Brad was gone, that's when I got this chunk
Of metal in my back. Well, you know, judge,

Getting blown up in the middle of the
Night changes your relationship
To sleep, so what Meg says is true: whenever

There's a noise at night I'm wide awake
Like that! Afterwards, when I was discharged,
Back at home, I had a little trouble

Readjusting—dreams, night sweats, things like that.
But, judge, that stuff about me crying
On the front stoop sounds like something from

A book. You've got to realize, your honor,
Mary Marg'ret's always felt like life should be
More meaningful, dramatic, than it

Is, or maybe could be, 's why she's always read
So much—novels mainly. Times she'd find
Descriptions in a book resembling how some

Rare thing that'd happened made her feel,
Sure enough, before you knew it, all
Those storybook emotions got mixed up there with

The truth, till she couldn't keep 'em straight,
That's when details from the book'd start
To be the things she'd recollect—

And how, I guess, I got to crying on
The steps. At any rate, anyone
Who knows Meg knows the way she's apt to make life

More romantic in the telling, no one
Thinks the less of her for that, and not, sir,
That I didn't have bad patches to get past

When I got back, things that I'd've had
A hard time handling without Meg there, urging
Me to go to college, get beyond

The stuff that I'd gone through. She said I saved
Her life that time she'd gotten so depressed
Miscarrying the second child. Well, maybe so,

But if I did, she gave me back
A life when I came home from 'Nam—that's no
Exaggeration, really. And isn't that

What marriage is supposed to do? Mary
Marg'ret always wanted what was best
For us, or for our kids, that's why when she

Had trouble carrying them to term, it hit her
Hard, and why, when Steve was born, I got
Concerned, sir, she'd have so much riding on

The boy psychologically, he might
Be hurt. You know, a mother-son relationship's
Always close anyway,

But Meg and Stevie shared so many int'rests,
Almost from the time he'd turned, say, eight
Or nine, that there were moments when we three'd

Be doing things together, judge, I felt
Like odd man out. Well, maybe that's extreme,
But still, I think you'd understand my

Saying sometimes, not that I was jealous
Of my son, but jealous of the time
That Meg would spend on Steve alone. Of course,

In those days I was working pretty hard,
Trying to make my mark down at the office,
So I guess I wasn't home as much as

Mary Marg'ret wanted. Later, when they
Gave me more responsibility,
I felt I had to justify their trust—

That's when I started going in at least
One day most weekends. See, I found I had
This talent motivating people, getting

All the folks I worked with pointing in
The same direction. Nothing that I know of's
So addictive, judge, as doing something

Difficult you're really good at. Me,
I'd never been that great in school, and after,
In the Corps, I'd mainly taken orders.

Still, I'd seen the kinds of officers
And noncoms got results, watched the way
They did it. So, in college when I changed

My major from accounting into business,
Well, I knew that managing a complex
Operation was the field where I was

Headed. What I liked about insurance
From the first was how it took
Predictability and hitched it to a wagon—

Making models with statistics,
Probabilities, actuarial tables,
Things like that. I think, sir, ever since

That tour overseas, I've had this
Apprehensiveness about the unexpected,
More like "unease," facing all the ways that

Randomness can put its oar in any
Time (some residue, I'd guess, of getting
Blown up in the dark). At any rate,

Working in insurance made me feel like
I could bring it, if not under rational
Control, at least within the scope

Of plain old forethought, made me feel more certain,
Thinking living wasn't just this muddling-
Through, by-guess-by-God affair I'd always

Feared. And as I said, sir, I was good
(More than good) when it came to solving
Problems, setting goals, getting folks

To work together. There's a sort of headiness
Comes with running your own shop,
Tuning people's wills so they resonate

With yours. I had my own division
Of the comp'ny by the time that I'd
Turned forty, then the deal with Allied

Came along and suddenly it seemed my
Big career was headed for the toilet.
If I got dropped when Allied bought us out,

I'd have to start from scratch with someone else,
I'd be behind the age curve there, career plans
Shot to hell. Maybe I was wrong, judge,

Letting this thing get to me the way
It did, wrong for letting so much of my sense
Of self get mixed up with my work,

But get to me it did, not that this
Excuses my involvement with that younger
Woman. I could say I went a little

Crazy, sure. I felt I couldn't talk
With Meg about the stuff at work, shouldn't
Worry her and Steve with what they couldn't change,

Not the way a man behaves and surely not
The way that I'd been raised. I felt
In some strange fashion if I told them how

Concerned I was about my maybe getting
Fired that this would only drive the two
Of them together more, leaving me alone,

Feeling somehow that I'd gone from being their
Protector suddenly to this big
Problem they'd both have to share—Daddy

On the dole. No, sir, I wasn't about
To show a sign of weakness to my wife
And son—my dad had taught me that. He hated

Weakness. So do I. And then I met
This woman at the office, facing similar
Uncertainties, needing no explanation

How it felt, and seeming, oddly
Enough, as much or more concerned about
My situation as her own—that's what

Attracted me at first, the way her whole
Attention, caring, focused just on me,
Not shared with someone else. Looking back,

I guess that must've been a trick, but at
The time, you know, she prob'bly sensed that that
Was what I needed, saw the way to save

Her job was pin her hopes on someone who'd
A better chance of getting through the merger,
Someone who could carry her along.

Although, to tell the truth, I didn't think
My chances were that good. Maybe she was
Playing me, your honor, but, you know,

One never blames that in a woman much,
Especially not a woman in the business world
Where the cards are stacked against them.

Yet how I could have let this thing turn sexual
Embarrasses me still, and yet
I did. I knew that it was wrong and, soon

Enough, saw it was crazy too. No excuse,
My fault entirely. When I broke it
Off, about the time the companies merged,

There wasn't anything, believe me, I
Could do to save the woman's job. Her whole
Subsection got rolled up. She took it badly,

But you know the rest. The night that Mary Marg'ret
Got her phone call seemed the hardest
Night in our whole marriage, though, of course,

I couldn't know then I'd a harder one
In store. I tried to tell her how ashamed
I was, how sorry, that I'd spend a lifetime

Making this thing up, showing her
How precious she and Stevie always were.
I said, "You know I've never been that kind of

Person, some skirt chaser. Can't you see
How desp'rate, stressed, I must've felt to do
A thing like that? That's not me." But, judge,

I guess you've noticed, hearing my wife's version,
She's an all-or-nothing kind of person.
Forgiving someone means you've got to meet them

Half way. When I saw she'd no intention,
Then, of doing that . . . , well, you know,
No one can expect another person

To abase himself completely and
Forever, so I figured, just back off,
Let time go by, maybe Mary Marg'ret

Needs some space to work this out. That's when,
Looking back, I made my big mistake,
I felt so bad about the way I'd hurt her,

Judge, that in effect I gave her Stevie
As a way to make amends, I mean
I stopped competing with her for the boy's

Affection, let her be the dominating
Force in Stevie's life. I thought that this'd
Fill the gap in her emotions made

By our estrangement, make her feel less lonesome
Maybe. But looking back, I wonder how I
Could've been so careless with my son,

About what Steve might need, the way he'd feel, sir,
Finding that his dad was taking less part
In his life, or how I could've used

A teenaged boy as buffer just to ease
His mother's angry sorrow over something
Bad his dad had done. I guess I must've

Thought since Steve and Meg had always been
So close, that this was something more in that
Direction? And maybe, though I don't much like

To think so, but just maybe, some resentment
Of that closeness got mixed in—perhaps
The feeling that if Steve preferred his mother,

I'd back off and let him have a double
Dose of her affection. Anyway,
I had my hands full at the office, heading

Up the same division once we'd been
Acquired. Before I knew it, my career had
Taken off again, and spending part

Of every weekend down at work was nothing
New at all. That's when the distance separating
Me and Meg began to harden.

I'd feel it mostly when the day was ending—
Like if we'd been out to dinner, maybe at some
Function for the comp'ny (more and

More of those as time went by), we'd get home late,
Go through that ritual married couples
Know by heart—she'd go upstairs to bed,

I'd take the garbage out, then check the back door
And the front, turn the outside floodlights on,
Then I'd go up, and she'd be fast

Asleep. Well, after that'd happened several
Times, I got to staying downstairs longer then,
Before I'd come to bed. I'd read

The paper, maybe have a drink, smoke
A cigarette, so when I'd climb the stairs,
She'd really be asleep. And gradually,

While this was going on, Stevie's int'rests,
His whole outlook, turned to things that struck me,
Sir, as odd, especially for a boy

His age—solitary pastimes, indoors,
Sedentary—int'rests (so it seemed
To me) he'd chosen just because I didn't

Share them. But who really knows what kids
Today are thinking? Then when he went through
That phase of staying in his room, playing

That same music endlessly (Meg says that
It was Gershwin, judge, but not like any
Show tune I remember), reading till

All hours, mostly novels (got that from his
Mother), well, I thought if he got sick the way
He did his senior year he'd see this sort

Of life just wasn't healthy, see he needed
Something that'd get him out of doors,
Maybe give the kid a rest from all

Those books, a breather after twelve straight years
In school. I knew that Steve was worried, thought
His being sick might stop him graduating

High school, keep him out of college, so
One evening after I got home from work,
Had dinner, well, I stopped by Stevie's room

Where he was still in bed recov'ring from
The flu, this three-day fever'd broke the night
Before. He lay there looking like a dishrag

Someone'd wrung out hard, I couldn't believe
How young he seemed. Maybe that's what led me,
Judge, to call him by his nickname, one

I hadn't used since Steve'd been a little
Fella: "Hey, Mac, how's the boy?" He murmured
In that gentle voice of his, "Better,

Dad." I said I knew how he'd been worrying
Over missing so much school, that maybe
He'd been putting too much pressure on

Himself, and what'd he think about his taking
Time off after high school, seeing something of
The world before he went to college,

Growing up a bit. That's when I said
He might consider, judge, a hitch in the Marines
Like his old man (I made it like

A joke, but wasn't joking), Stevie knew that,
So he waited just a moment, then
He said he didn't think the Corps would want

Someone like him. I told him don't be silly,
Grandpa fought at Iwo, I was at
Khe Sanh, the Corps knew things like that were in

The blood, he'd sprung from royalty the way they'd
See it. Stevie lay back on his pillow
Looking weary, closed his eyes, said he'd

Think about it. Well, he must've talked it
Over with his mother, 'cause a day
Or two later Mary Marg'ret gave me hell:

Asked me was I crazy, fixing
To get her son blown up, keep him out
Of college. Why'd we worked so hard raising

Ourselves up above our parents not to
Have our only child go higher still?
I said that Stevie'd get more out of college

After being on his own a while,
Be more mature, know what he wanted. Mary
Marg'ret seemed to feel, sir, I was saying

This to hurt her, so I let the matter
Drop. That's when she started helping Stevie
Every day to catch up on the things

He'd missed in school, almost as if she wanted
To show me up. At any rate when he got
Well and finished high school, sure enough

His mood improved, seemed he felt like going
Off to college cleared his head. Of course,
Mary Marg'ret missed him badly. Nothing

I could do would alter that. She called him
Ev'ry day or so at first. And then that
Christmas break—my God! he'd changed. We had

This talk down in the study, judge, he said
He'd stopped attending classes, felt
He'd lost his way, that maybe working outdoors

With his hands was what he needed. Sure,
I said, that's the reason I'd suggested
Stevie's trying the Marines, but now he'd

Started college it would break his mother's
Heart dropping out his freshman year,
(Besides the fact she'd think I'd had a hand

In this). I made a deal with Steve: finish
Out the school year, get the credit, then
We'd see about his working for the summer

Landscape gardening, seeing how he liked it.
Then, judge, if he felt the same way still,
We'd both discuss it with his mother. Also,

I reminded him they gave degrees in landscape
Architecture, forestry, stuff
Like that (though maybe not at State)

So if he really meant to do this right,
He'd have to go to college. That's the way
We left it. Steve went back next morning, saying

He'd some studying still to do. And maybe
If I'd listened closer, heard the pain
Behind the words, I'd've understood

What Stevie tried to tell me . . . maybe. Lots
Of maybes, judge, but when the phone rang that next
Night they'd all become the distant past.

There was a moment there after I heard
The news, I flashed back to that night in 'Nam
Brad got cut in two. You know, judge, memory's

In the muscles much as in the mind,
I had the same sensation then, this muscular
Feeling, helpless, hopeless, dragging arms

And legs down like lead weights, the same as when
They told me Steve was dead. I had to call
His uncle Pat. I knew I'd wreck the car

Trying to drive that night, then all that long way
Down to College Park when Meg says she was
Thinking how they could've got the boy's name wrong,

This same picture kept returning:
Out in 'Nam, often when we'd capture
VC prisoners, judge, we'd give them to

The Arvin for "intelligence extraction."
Well, those boys played pretty rough. They'd take
The dinks up, two or three a time, couple of

Thousand feet above the jungle in a
Chopper, start in questioning them there and if
They didn't get the stuff they wanted,

Toss one out the door—that way the other
Birds'd realize, the sarge'd wisecracked,
"Either they'd have to sing or learn to fly."

You'd look up every time you heard a chopper's
Whup-whup-whup, thinking maybe you might see
Some little guy in black pajamas, upper

Arms wired behind him, sailing out
A Huey's door. The falling seemed to take
Forever from that height, though I'd think to myself,

It wouldn't seem that long at all, if you were
Guest of honor. Thing was, judge, that when
They'd fall their upper bodies were immobile,

Wired real tight, but from the waist down, hands
And legs kept thrashing, flailing (as if that
Could make a diff'rence). Prob'bly just a reflex,

Trying to get their arms up, shield their face
And head. You'd see them vanish in the tree line,
Maybe hear them crashing through the limbs and

Vines, if you were close enough. This one time,
Judge, (and here's the picture kept returning
On that drive to College Park) we'd crossed this

Dry creek bed out on patrol (a solid
Rock plateau), and here's this dink lying
Face down looking like he's fast asleep—

Except the odd position of his arms.
We figured from the body's state he hadn't
Been there long—he'd swelled a little,

Blackened some, skin covered with black flies.
First thing we did was check to see if he was
Mined, he wasn't, so we figured how we'd

Got there first, before the VC had.
That's when we thought we'd booby-trap him, give his
Friends a nice surprise if they dropped by.

Well, when we went to lift him (Bradshaw had him
By the arms, I had him by the ankles),
Sure enough, soon as we picked him up

His underside fell out, just like a wet
Paper sack. Maybe the impact did it,
Maybe the maggots loosened him up. At any

Rate, we cleared the guts away, then put
A Bouncing Betty in his abdomen,
Wedged the spring against the backbone, left

Him sleeping for his pals to find. Well, that's
The scene kept coming back driving down
To College Park. I thought about that young man

In the jungle (did I mention, judge,
The dink was in his teens?), I thought about
The way he died, that long agonizing

Fall, and how he must've had a father,
Some poor farmer who'd be brokenhearted
Learning his first son was dead (that's if he

Ever did), a man who'd never know how his boy's
Body, in the hands of careless
Strangers, turned to bait to maim his friends.

Why that came to mind then's something I've
Thought lots about, sir, since that night. Not that
I'd expected Stevie's body'd be

Split open like that other from the fall
(It wasn't far enough), no, rather, just
The thought my only son was in the hands

Of people who, no matter how benevolent
Their work, would handle him like any other
Stiff found in the streets—not that precious,

Personal quantity Meg and I had loved,
The thought I'd have to claim my son from strangers
Who'd've done this sort of job so often,

Judge, that even if their feelings for
The grief most people suffered showing up
Retrieving bodies had been real the first

Few times, by now mere self-defense had made all
Personal responses mostly rote.
Thinking back about that evening now,

I catch myself imagining an old man
Standing in a rice field just at dusk,
Ankle deep in water, finding, after

So much stooping, standing straight is hard,
And longing for some younger man to come
And help. I guess, judge, no one ever does

Outrun his past, things always even up.
Well, the rest of what that night was like
You heard from Meg. Where I was paralyzed

More or less after hearing Steve
Was dead, Meg was all for action, sure
They'd misidentified the boy, we had

To go right down there. Well, when we showed up
And Meg first saw Steve lying on that gurney,
All at once we seemed to switch positions,

She collapsed, and just as quick I started
Organizing things, talking to
The ambulance attendants, then the cops,

The doctor who'd first worked on Steve, I had
To make arrangements where they'd take the body
Once the autopsy was done, which funeral

Home, and then the Mass, the catering for
The wake—that's what kept me busy the next
Few days, kept me sane. I tried involving

Mary Marg'ret in the planning, judge,
Hoping having something real to do
Would snap her out of it, but no. She spent

The days before the funeral weeping constantly—
That or else sedated. I stayed away from
Work, long as I could, trying to help her

Get back on her feet. She kept repeating
How it must've been an accident—
Didn't I think so? I finally felt

I had to tell her what the cop'd said—
About the door lock being taped—but then she
Said he could've just gone up there for

The air, taking a break, maybe he'd
Been drinking, maybe he'd been smoking something.
That's what the cops had thought—alcohol

Or drugs. But, you see, I'd seen the autopsy
Report, and, well . . . , *those* things weren't in his
        blood.
But I decided not to tell her that—

She'd only feel, sir, I was being difficult,
So I thought, let her think it
Was an accident if that'll get her

Past the worst. Well, within six weeks
She had this breakdown, first the hospital,
Then the private sanatorium, in

And out, back and forth. That time she entered
Ridgecrest for the second stay within
Six months I nearly gave up hope. I'd work

All day, then grab a bite to eat before
I'd make the long drive out there to the home,
Sometimes she'd be better, sometimes not—

No predicting. I remember when I'd
Come back late at night from visiting,
How the house would seem so empty, almost like

Nobody'd ever lived there. I'd fix myself
A Scotch, sink down in that wing chair in
The study, snapping on the reading lamp

But leaving all the rest in darkness, start
To think about the way events fall out,
Wond'ring why it happened, when that rocket-

Propelled grenade blew up our slit trench thirty
Years ago, that it was Brad got cut
In two not me, or what the tables showed

About young men who'd killed themselves their first
Semester into college. Then, since I was
Trying every trick to stun my mind,

Get it tired enough to sleep, I'd think back
Far as I could go, starting with
The big bang, estimating all the combinations,

Judge, the great machine had run through
(Millions upon millions), hurtling down blind
Channels chance would open, seeking ways

To tilt the whole array—those lighted, lazy
Spirals turning soundlessly in space—then
Tip it up a notch, while time resumed its

Patient sifting of the stars. Yes, looking
Back along its length now, it might seem
Like one long chain of choices, hammered out

From fewest links (inevitable—say even
Elegant), right decisions nature'd
Come on, though we know at ev'ry moment

On its way it could've turned out diff'rent,
Certain that no matter how exacting,
Economic, this long chain might seem,

Its making took, if one counts single things,
Enormous cost across the ages just to
Bring it down to one tired man who's sitting in a

Darkened room, then place that chain's end
Gently in his hand, a man who in
A year or so'll be his comp'ny's

Youngest-ever president, whose only child
Committed suicide the year he turned
Eighteen, whose wife collapsed and wouldn't be

The same again, sir, once she'd gotten strange
Ideas she had to empty out her life
As this memorial, this testament

To how much, judge, she'd loved her son, to how
His death had drained her life of meaning. Well,
This man who's sitting in the dark, fingering

The chain's end, wonders whether these
Three lives and how they've turned out represent that
Brutal sifting still at work. That's when

He feels how light the chain is, how contingent
At its ev'ry link, what a slender
Thing a life is, knowing all the while

It binds him tighter than one could predict,
Considering its weight. Well, your honor,
That's the sort of thing I thought about

Those late nights in that lonesome house, until I'd
Either fall asleep there in the wing chair
Or the morning's icy light would send

Me climbing up the stairs to shave and shower,
Head back down to work. It was work
That kept me sane through all that time, hard work,

And knowing quitting never was an option.
At any rate when Meg'd been released
That last time from the psychiatric ward

She had her plans already made: she'd leave her
Former life behind with all its disappointments,
Aching sorrows—'cept for one.

And, sure enough, the representative
Of all that hurtful stuff was you-know-who.
Well, sir, we know what marriage is, the way

A spouse becomes with passing time a stand-in
For the world, the one who makes it wear
A human face, so if you've been ignored by life,

Mistreated, suffered some reverse,
Why then there's one who'll treat your case with some
Respect, the simple dignity ev'ry

Human's got a right to. Well, I tried
Explaining this to Meg, explaining how, sir,
Just because a husband fills this role

Of smiling substitute, stunt double for the world,
She mustn't ever get the two of them
Mixed up, mustn't think if life

Hauls off and kicks her in the shins, her husband
Somehow secretly condones it, maybe's
Personally at fault. A spouse, I said,

Can listen for the world, but look, that doesn't
Mean he speaks for it, takes its side.
Besides, the things she'd suffered, judge, I'd suffered

Too—well, maybe not the younger woman
Part, but still, I suffered longer for that after,
Just in a diff'rent way. I told her

That. Mary Marg'ret sat there silent
For a bit, then said, "It's all just talk.
Ev'ry time we talk, and you begin

To 'reason,' Bill, I lose. So I'm not having
Any of it, no." I said Steve's death
Was something neither of us ever would

Get over. Still, would Steve have wanted that
To break us up? I said I didn't think so.
We'd lost our only child, we'd never have

Another, all there'd ever be of him
In *this* world was the mem'ries, fragile pictures
That'd stand the strongest chance of lasting

With the ones who'd always loved him best,
And long as we could find in one another
Traces of the way he'd looked and sounded,

Steve still lived, the link that held us both.
Or I wondered out loud, was it that she
Didn't even want to share Steve's mem'ry

With me? All she'd say was "There are things
    that break
That can't be fixed." Well, judge, I guess
That's all I know to say. The fact I'm here

Today contesting this divorce, pursuing
One last chance, I'm hoping shows Meg just
How much she means to me. Still, if she

Persists in wanting to be free, there's nothing
I can do, I'll have to let her go.
I'll try to handle it the way I did with

Stevie's death, I'll lose myself in work,
But I know me, the loneliness'll start
To wear me out, the eating meals alone,

The waking up alone at night, and so,
Predictably, I'll find a new companion,
Prob'bly someone younger—that's the way

These things work out most often. Lord have mercy!
Just the thought of dating after fifty
Fills me with ridiculous despair,

Imagining the sort of things one says
On first dates, all the not-so-subtle self-
Advertisements you need to make, the reasons

You're a catch, although you're more than twenty
Years her senior. And then, you know, there're
     all those
Little tests you have to go through

Just to show the girl you're still "a fun-type
Guy." But if you never were a fun-type
Guy . . . , well, how do you begin? Dancing

Lessons? Dye your hair? Whole new wardrobe?
And how does one describe that situation—
Mainly pitiful, mostly abject, judge,

Or what? Almost worse than being lonely,
But not quite. I'm hoping Mary Marg'ret's
Got enough residual affection

Left she'd never let her Billy come
To that. But maybe not. Whatever happens
Now, I'm holding out until there's no more hope—

And maybe, judge, just a bit beyond.
Thank you for your candor, Mr.
Fish. Indeed, thank you both. Well, Mrs. Fish,

What's it going to be? Has any
Of what Mr. Fish's said here made a dent
In your intention to divorce?

VII

I know Bill hopes I'll change my mind, thinks
I'm being foolish, even crazy, feels like
I've abandoned him, that loneliness'll

Drive him to the arms of some young girl
Dead set on dancing Billy's feet off ev'ry
Night. Say, listen, who's he kidding? Men

Are such big babies, judge. And they call us
The weaker sex. We're tougher when it comes
To standing pain (if not, who'd have their kids?).

And since the figures show how many years
We're destined to outlive them, we've developed
Thicker skins when it comes to being

Lonely, knowing older women mostly
End up by themselves. It's not that Bill
Can't handle being lonely if I leave,

It's that he doesn't want to spend the time
Building up a private life again without
Me there, he doesn't want the change,

Some break in his routine deflecting his
Attention from that blesséd comp'ny, judge,
No pers'nal obligations interfering

With his role as "single-minded CEO
Bill Fish." Bill said he hoped I'd still
Some old affection left. Well, sure, the Billy

That I fell in love with thirty years
Ago'll prob'bly never leave my heart,
But after what I've gone through since Steve died,

I wonder how Bill thinks that I could help him,
When it isn't even clear, sir, I can help
Myself. It's like you're shipwrecked, floating

In the water clinging to debris
(A plank, a broken crate), trying to keep
Your head up when you hear somebody calling "Help."

You know, if you call back, that they'll
Swim over, then the added weight'll likely
Sink you both. The only way to save them's

Wait till they get near, then push the crate
In their direction, wave good-bye, and swim away
Yourself, looking for some other raft

To cling to. Don't know, your honor, if that
Tells you what I feel, I only know that
If we stayed together Bill and I would

Drown for sure. I've got to swim away.
He's got his raft down at the office. Me,
I'll keep on swimming off and out of sight.

It may not seem like much, sir, when it comes
To plans, but it's the only one I've got.
I'm sticking to it now—no matter what.

Well, Mrs. Fish, if that's your final word.
I must say list'ning to you both I had
The sense I've had so often here before,

That life, filled as it is with trouble, sudden
Heartbreak, sorrows of all sorts, is way
Too much for each to face alone,

Indeed, a sense of what first drove our kind to seek
Lifelong alliances by twos against
The stalking darkness, aching cold, the anguished

Loneliness that we each fear and feel
And fight to mitigate by reaching out
A hand at night in bed, and yet a separateness

We end up loving more than hating when it's
Reckoned as the cost of ev'ry
Soul's uniqueness, necessary carfare

If the self's to stay completely mobile
To its moods. And frankly, if you think
About it, who among us hasn't felt

The need, one time or another, just to walk
Away and leave his life behind,
As much to say, "I'm more than all the things

I have, more than anything I do.
That's nothing but the shell time's drifting sands've
Cased me in." But if you walk away,

What then? Anywhere you stop, the clock
Restarts, the sands accumulate again.
And can you leave your life each day, time after

Time? I know how some folks, married lots of
Years, 'll often feel this desp'rate urge
To chuck it all, start their lives from scratch,

Distracted beings balanced all their days
Along the knife-edge thrust between their dread
Of isolation and their longing for such freedom.

You know, I think that's our defining fate—
That and needing someone else as lost
As we to share it with. Sometimes I really

Think I've done this sort of thing too long,
Been privy to more suff'ring than a single
Life's allowed, presiding over time's great

Grinding wheel going round, wearing out
One's early hopes, affections, crushing them
To powder more dispersed in air

Than dust motes circling through a sudden sunbeam
As it slants across a hot and musty
Room. Your time's a killer, yes, make no

Mistake, and yet say this for time: live long
Enough, it frees you from the fever of
That loneliest illusion—what Mrs. Fish'd

Called the dream of love. Afraid I know
Firsthand of what I speak, know all too well.
But as I say, I've done this sort of work

Too long. So if your mind's made up then, Mrs.
Fish, there's nothing left but set a date and
Bring the suit to trial. My clerk'll check

Availabilities, then notify
Your lawyers. Still, before we break this up,
I'd like to settle if I can this matter

Of the sister who (I'd guess from what
Our Mr. Fox reported here before this
Hearing'd begun) is more than likely

In the custody of bailiffs, cuffed
And waiting just outside that door right now.
So then, since at least two people in this

Room have grounds for bringing charges where
The sister is concerned, I'd just as soon not
Have a pending criminal matter muddying

Waters, don't you see?, when Fish v. Fish
Proceeds to trial, creating diff'rent sorts
Of tensions with the parties and their lawyers.

With that said then, Mr. Fish, are you
Intent on pressing charges over those events
Occurring earlier in the hall?

No, your honor. Don't see how I'd ever have
A chance convincing Mary Marg'ret
She should change her mind about divorce

If all the while I'm getting set to toss her
Sister in the slammer. 'Sides these little
Dustups with Gert Fallon go back years,

They started when we both were kids, about the
Time when Gert decided, judge, I wasn't
Good enough to tie her sister's shoe.

Well, Mr. Fish, I think you've made a wise
Decision. If I might suggest, would you
And Mrs. Fish and Mr. Bird just step

Outside a moment? I'd like to try and clear
The air between your sister-in-law and Mr.
Fox. Thank you. . . . Well now, Fox, I don't

See how—once your client has declined
To press a criminal charge against the sister,
Feeling this would prejudice attempts

At straight'ning things out with his wife—I say
I don't see how, Fox, as his lawyer, you'd be
Able to proceed against the lady

On your own. Now, of course, if you
Press charges, you could always then recuse
Yourself from representing Fish in court,

On grounds your interests and your client's
Were at odds. But that would mean, you see,
Your client would require another lawyer,

With a consequent reduction in your
Fee. That's why I'm betting, Fox, that if
I get the sister in here, have her allocute

To those infractions in the hall, then make
A full and frank and free . . . And humble. Yes,
"And humble," Fox, apology for all

Her insults to your person, surely you might
Reconsider your intention earlier
Expressed to throw her in the jug.

Well, since you put it that way, judge,
I might incline to lenience where the sister
Is concerned, that's if the dame's apology

Is full and frank and free and humble—also
Heartfelt and sincere. *Don't push it, Fox.*
Just step outside and ask the bailiffs, if you

Would, to bring the lady in. Very well,
Your honor, but be careful, she's
A menace. . . . Biggs, Dobbs, conduct the prisoner

To the bar. *Ah, Mr. Biggs, Mr.*
Dobbs, come in. And this must be Ms. Fallon.
How do you do? Sure an' I'm mussed a bit—

But nothing next to these two. *Biggs, do we*
Really need the handcuffs on Ms. Fallon?
Well, sir, if you knew how much it took

To get 'em on her. *Something of a tussle,*
Was it? Lord! monumental is
The way that I'd describe it. See, when Mr.

Fox here came and found me, sayin' how
He'd been assaulted, battered, ditto for
His client, well, we set out lookin' for the

Perp, and sure enough, we're searchin' through
The halls, turn a corner, all at once
He sees her, freezes in his tracks like that!,

Then motions with his head "That's her." Well now,
You know, judge, I'm not young like what I used
To be—matter of fact, I'm due retirement

Three years come June, so when I saw the
        perpetrator's
Size, I went and got young Dobbs,
Who's big and strong and full of you-know-what

And vinegar—besides the fact he's always
Been a joker, so I figures this here
Gal'll take him down a peg. Well, sir,

We turn into the hall where I last seen her,
All at once Dobbs here gets the giggles,
So I says, "You, Dobbs, straighten up!" And he says,

Playin' dumb just like he does, "Which one
Is it?" I says, "Dobbs, you joker, which d'ya
Think? That there—the one looks like she'd swallowed

Burl Ives." Well, Dobbsie really gets
To gigglin' then, so I says, "Dobbs, you're gonna
Earn your pay today." As we're approachin' her,

She yells, "So, they've sent the Black and
Tans." Well, judge, I'm blacker by a lot
Than Dobbs, but ain't no way no one could call him

"Tan." So I thinks, Whoa!, we gots a regular
Looney on our hands. We try arrestin' her
And right away the scufflin' starts.

I get my arm around her head, sir, from
Behind, but she gets Dobbsie's head same way
(She's big, judge, but she's quick.) She tries to break

My headlock with a sit out (must've done
Some wrestlin', seems), but I hold on and go down
With her. Well, of course, she takes young Dobbs

Down too. So now the three of us're sandwiched
On the floor, me the bread, this great big gal
The ham, and Dobbs the mustard. Dobbs'd

Almost got his cuff around the wrist what's
Wedged up against his throat when all at once
She breaks the other hand free (told you she

Was quick), grabs Dobbsie by the crotch, twists his
Joystick so he makes a noise just like
A screech owl (nothin' like you ever heard

Bust out a growed man's mouth before). Well, Dobbs
Was out of action, judge, (and just between us two,
That boy ain't gonna walk right for a week).

I had her by the neck still, but I couldn't
Do no more. Dobbs had rolled off in a corner
Moanin', I was gettin' winded,

Collar seemed in doubt, when suddenly two more
Bailiffs, Potts and Bates, come runnin' up,
And she says, "Gawd! More Black and Tans!" Well, you

Know Potts and Bates, sir, both of them are white boys,
That's the instant that I yells to Dobbs,
"This gal is nuts!" And if she's not, judge, let me

Tell you, she's sure got that thing we call
In law enforcement "crazy-strength." Well, me
And Potts and Bates were finally able then to

Get the handcuffs on her (Dobbs was
Mostly ruined). We got her on her feet, got her
Dusted off, then helped Dobbs here so's he

Could stand up straight, without he make those
Little yippin' noises. That's when we brought her
Back and had her waitin' just outside, sir,

'Cause I knowed you'd want to see what caused
The rumpus. Thing is, judge, all the time
We're waitin', she keeps starin' in my eyes

Like we're heavyweights before a fight,
Seein' will I blink or look away.
And every time she looks at Dobbs, he gives

This high-pitched groan and shuts his eyes.
    That's cold.
This gal's the bluin' on gun metal, judge.
If I was you, I'd leave the cuffs stay on.

Well, Mr. Biggs, let me first commend
Both you and Mr. Dobbs for action far
Above the line of duty. Indeed, Biggs, after

Hearing your account of what occurred,
I'm taking Fox's fine suggestion that I
Put a letter noting this performance

In your files in personnel. Now,
About the other matter, I appreciate
Your real concern for safety, still Ms. Fallon

Seems subdued enough, Biggs, after your
Colossal hand-to-hand exertions, so I
Think I'd rather have the handcuffs off.

That seems the proper note to strike in seeking
Reconciliation, trying if we
Can to mend whatever breach of peace

Occurred between our Mr. Fox and this
Large debutante. Yes, take the bracelets off—
Providing that, Ms. Fallon, I've your word

Of honor not to lose your temper nor
Provoke the sort of contretemps transpiring
Earlier in the hall. You've got my word

On that one, judge. By gawd! I don't know what
False lies this Mr. Fox has told about me here
Behind my back, but I don't even know, sir,

How to do a "country stomp."
No, sir, the step I did on Foxy there's
What's known as hard-shoe dancing 'cross the sea

In Ireland. As for me "perspiring," well,
I've always had that problem—that's no crime.
But, judge, I promise, I won't break the peace.

Since I've your word on that, Ms. Fallon, freely
Given, go ahead and take the cuffs off, Mr.
Biggs, then you and Mr. Dobbs

Can step outside. All right, your honor. There,
She's loose. But Dobbs and me'll be outside
That door—if you should hafta call for help.

As you see fit. . . . Now, Ms. Fallon, let me
Tell you why we brought you in here. Mr.
Fox, as you may know, alleges that you

Roughed him up (indeed, both him and Mr.
Fish) a while ago outside this door.
Your brother-in-law declines to bring a charge,

And Fox says he's content to let the matter
Drop if you'll admit your actions, then
Apologize, you see, and do it fully, frankly,

Freely, also humbly and sincerely.
Don't forget "and in a heartfelt manner."
Ah yes, "and in a heartfelt manner." Now, Ms.

Fallon, I'd advise compliance, seeing
That's the quickest way to get the matter
Settled. Tell us if you will what happened,

Triggering this dispute with Mr. Fox.
Well, judge, I came here planning to support
My baby sister when she entered this

First hearing, so she'd see a friendly face,
Going in and coming out. But seems
I must've got the time all wrong, 'cause I

Show up, and it's too early's what the guy
Outside there says. So I sit down to wait,
Then take a stroll, come back, and pretty soon

Bill Fish turns up, acting hoity-toity,
Sniffing all around, the way he does
At meals, then sits down on the bench—other

End, of course, far away as he
Can get. I says, "'Fraid I'll bite you, Bill?"
And he says, "No, not since you've had your
    rabies shot."

That gets it going, tit for tat, give as
Good as you get, till Bill Fish makes this gesture, when
I've got to smack him down—once,

Maybe twice, nothing big. I walk
Away, and as I'm coming back I see
These folks around where Bill is kneeling. Well,

This bald guy's yawping like he'd wrote the book
Of martyrs, wants to know what monster did this
Thing, what fiend from hell'd knocked the holy

Crap out of his client. Well, I tiptoed
Up behind him, reached around with one hand,
Got his tie, the other took his collar wing,

Then I shook him just a little
So's he'd know not to go calling people
Fiends without a proper introduction.

Well, Fox, does that sound roughly like what happened?
Ask her, judge, if she'd been drinking when
She got here—why it was, when she grabbed me

From behind, I damn near fainted dead away there
From the smell of rock and rye?
Well, Ms. Fallon, what about it? Is this

True, what Mr. Fox is saying now?
Sure an' I've had a terrible cold here lately,
Judge, settled in my chest, makes me

Cough something awful, that's why when I got
Ready to come down here, knowing what
Lace pants these legal fellas are, I thought

I couldn't have a coughing fit, maybe end up
Hawking in a hankie, so I
Poured myself a toddy 'fore I came.

Then when I got here early, judge, I sat
Outside a while, then took a little walk.
Well, there's this bar just down the street, I think

It's called the Sink . . . *I think you mean the Zinc.*
Ain't that what I said? Well, anyway,
The barman there's this old Eye-talian fella,

Hears me coughing, says he's got the very
Thing to fix me up. Well, 'fore you know it,
Judge, I had a dose, and then another

(That guinea's cure worked like a charm) and why I
Couldn't cough now if I tried. That's when
I came back here and waltzed with Mr. Fox.

*Well, Ms. Fallon, let me say, you seem
Restored to health, a twinkle in your eye,
Roses in both cheeks (perhaps a shade there*

*On your nose), one fine figure of
A woman in the very prime of life,
I'd say.* You can call me Gert. *Ah, well, I don't . . .*

Your honor, she's been drinking, she herself
Admits it: Ipsa dixit, ipso
Facto. *Fox* . . . Say, who's this Orangeman callin'

"Tipsy fatso"? *Now, Ms. Fallon . . . Keep it
Up there, Foxy. Run your mouth, and you and me'll
Dance just one more time. Ms. Fallon,*

*Please. We're trying here to solve
This situation, mollify hurt feelings,
Keep this gentleman from pressing charges.*

*Besides, there's still the matter of your own
Apology.* Never mind, your honor.
Don't I know when I've been threatened? What's it

Mean to say we'll "dance another time"
Except she's aims to lie in wait outside
And, when we're through here, spring, and bite me in

The shorts. Well, your honor, let me tell you,
Nothing she could say would save her now.
And when it comes to threats, they don't impress me.

I simply quote the sly Noel Coward who, sir,
Sitting in a bar on Capri, used to
Cry out when Kraut tourists there'd stare at him

With cruel eyes, "Finiculi,
Finicula, finic-yourself!" *Now, Fox!*
That does it, judge. Let me at the little . . .

Ms. Fallon! Please! Come here, Foxy, there's a
Word I wanna whisper in your ear.
Mr. Fox, just back away—that's it,

Get behind me. Step aside, your worship.
Now, Ms. Fallon! Don't you do it, judge!
Fox, stay where you are, keep backing up.

I'm running out of room, there's a
Wall back here, you know! *Now, Ms. Fallon,*
Don't do anything you might regret!

Your eminence, if you won't move, I'll have
To reach an arm around on either side
And grab a hold of Mr. Fox like that.

Ms. Fallon! Help me, judge! She's got me by
The shoulders of the coat! Try to push her
Off! *I'm trying, Fox. My arms are pinned,*

She's shoved herself so close against me . . . Oof!
That I can hardly breathe. Her hands! They're giant
Crabs! They're creeping down my sides! They're past

The belt! They're headed for my, oh my God!
She means to yank my johnson off! Help me!
Mayday! *What, Fox?!* . . . AARRGH! *Ms. Fallon, I think*

I'm passing out. Biggs, Biggs! I need you! Now!
Here I am, your honor. My God! she's treed 'em
Both. You, Dobbs, get in here! It's that rematch

You been wantin'. Get around there on that
Other side, use your Mace. Careful
How you hold that can, you got our Mr.

Fox there with that last one. That's it, spray her good.
Now get her wrist, get the cuff on tight,
Pull her arm behind her back. There,

That's the other cuff. Now put her in a
Chair, and help me with the judge. Lay him up here
On the desk. Now, Dobbs, you see

To Mr. Fox, he's lookin' like he might
Be sick. Oh, Lord! Look away, Dobbs. Poor Mr.
Fox done whupped his breakfast in the judge's

Leather chair. Get some water. Help me
Loosen up the judge's collar. Take his
Tie off. Here, just sprinkle that right on his

Face. I'll pinch his cheeks, pull his ears.
Say somethin', judge, say somethin'. Lord!, if this
Gal's killed the boss, there goes my pension sure.

I told him. Didn't I tell him? Wait! He's movin',
Sayin' somethin'. *I, uh* . . . Yes, judge? *I, uh* . . .
What, judge? *I, uh* . . . *think that I'm in love.*